PORTALS
OF THE MIND

ALSO BY STEPHEN WISE

<u>Short Story Collection</u>

The Signpost Up Ahead

<u>Individual Short Stories</u>

Another Stupid Time Travel Trip

Electronic Telepathy

Ode de la Lune

The Barn

The Melting Man

The Poem

<u>Screenplays</u>

Batman DarKnight (with Lee Shapiro)

Paradigm (with Eric Kaplan)

Maelstrom

PORTALS
OF THE MIND

A SHORT STORY COLLECTION

STEPHEN WISE

ARROWHEAD
PUBLICATIONS

HUMAN
AUTHORED
Authors Guild
4229542

For Uncle Bruce

You constantly presented me with new ideas while I was growing up and challenged my way of looking at the world. You live on in my memory.

Fiction, imaginative work that is, is not dropped like
a pebble upon the ground, as science may be; fiction
is like a spider's web, attached ever so lightly
perhaps, but still attached to life at all four corners.

— VIRGINIA WOLF

CONTENTS

PREFACE

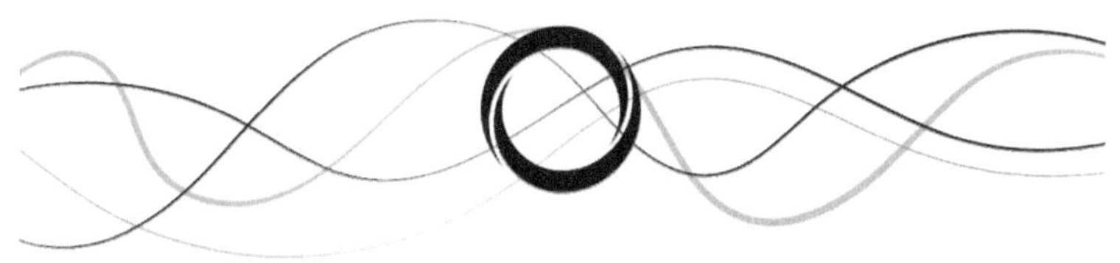

From the time I was quite small, I loved reading books and watching movies and TV. I spent more time thinking about fictional universes than reality, and I knew that when I grew up, I wanted to share my own stories with the world, either through print or a visual medium.

Early in life, I discovered the joy of expressing myself through the written word. While in elementary school, I taught myself how to type on an old manual Underwood typewriter (for anyone born after 1990, typewriters are those clunky mechanical things that look like computer keyboards without monitors) and plinked out as many stories as my young mind could think up. In addition to writing prose, I tried my hand at plays and movie scripts.

During these formative years, my older brother Kenny introduced me to two TV shows that made a strong and lasting impact—*Monty Python's Flying Circus* and *The Twilight Zone*. The comedians of Monty Python taught me about non sequiturs, wit blurred with silliness, and wild, free-form imagination. Rod Serling showed me how to surprise the audience with twist endings, weave meaningful themes into plots, and think beyond what you can experience with your normal senses. Both shows embraced and celebrated short form storytelling—demonstrating how to tell a complete tale with depth, emotion, and surprise in a limited amount of time.

During my teen years, I found great pleasure in a current (albeit short-lived) crop of anthology television: a new version of *Twilight Zone*, an updated *Alfred Hitchcock Presents*, *Amazing Stories*, *Tales from the Darkside*, *Tales from the Crypt*, *Monsters*, *Freddy's Nightmares*, and so on. Publications such as Omni, Isaac Asimov's Science Fiction Magazine, the Magazine of Science Fiction and Fantasy, and Twilight Zone Magazine (notice a repeating pattern?) grabbed hold of my imagination, as did volumes of short stories by Stephen King, Ray Bradbury, Roald Dahl, and others.

While studying screenwriting in college, I churned out scores of short stories that I recently re-discovered in boxes stored away. One day, I'll dust some of them off and add a coat of polish in order to prepare them for publication. Two of these older works, "The Last Stand at the Bellmont Mission" and "The Musician," made it into this collection. I originally wrote them as gifts to my parents, and they are obviously special to me.

Longer works are wonderful (I love epics like King's *The Stand* and Tolkien's *Lord of the Rings*), but short fiction is a literary form that I cherish. As a filmmaker, I have written, directed, and produced about a dozen short films. As an author, I have chosen ten stories (and one poem) to share with you in this anthology. I hope you enjoy them.

—Stephen Wise, December 6, 2014

A decade after this book was originally published, I decided to dust it off and give it a facelift. This includes a new cover and interior design, but also a re-edit with fresh eyes. The content of the stories have not changed, but the grammar and sentence structures have been cleaned up for a smoother read.

Having gone through these stories again after so long, I have to admit that I enjoy them and even surprised myself with some details I had forgotten. Certain aspects of the stories are now dated (who owns a digital camera anymore when we have them on our phones?), but I don't see the need to update any references. These are a product of their time and should be kept as such.

I hope this eclectic collection entertains you, the reader.

—Stephen Wise, January 26, 2024

THE PORTALS

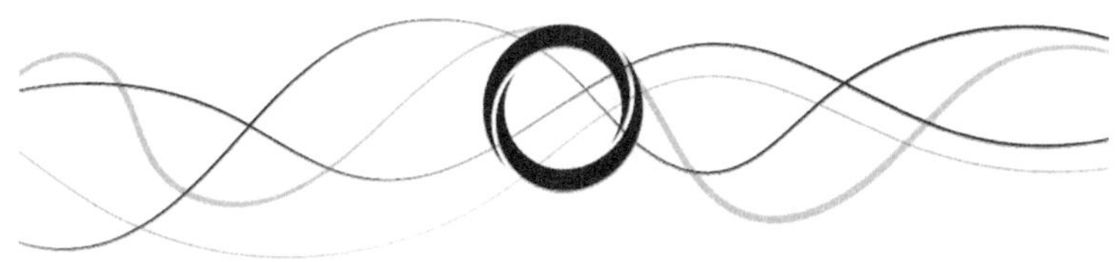

"See those little circles there? Those are portals to another dimension."

Max looked at his uncle with incredulousness.

At fourteen, Max loved all things fantastical—he had a collection of Piers Anthony and Terry Brooks novels; *Lord of the Rings* played incessantly on his DVD player (his mom refused to buy the Blu-ray set, considering its redundancy unnecessary and too costly despite Max's protest to the contrary); and a large percentage of his free time (too much, according to his dad) was dedicated to *World of Warcraft*. He proudly proclaimed his geekdom at school and kept a constant vigil for a new excursion into the realm of imagination.

Still, he knew the difference between fantasy and the real world. He'd love to ride a winged hippogriff across the sunset or journey through the galaxy in the Millennium Falcon, but he knew he was just a kid from Houston. The closest he would get to space travel was taking a field trip to the Johnson Space Center. He would never be an astronaut as he was terrible at math, and his interest in science leaned toward figuring out how things burned or exploded.

"Portals to another dimension?" Max repeated, trying to keep disbelief out of his voice. He liked his uncle and didn't want to hurt his feelings. Regardless, he knew the man had a habit of going off the deep end with strange ideas. When Max was little, he loved hearing about aliens who visited the Earth centuries ago and bred the human species, or how houses built from metal would generate a healing magnetic field, or that there was a hole in the Earth's core at the North Pole that planes would fly into and disappear. These conversations would go on for hours, sparking the boy's imagination.

The problem, of course, was that Max was now growing up and understood what was factual and what wasn't. He hadn't become cynical—not yet—but his mind was becoming set regarding the world around him, which was tangible and often unpleasant. Bigfoot existed no more than the Bermuda Triangle or the end of the world, as the Mayan calendar predicted.

"Portals." Bob Gutermuth's eyes held a steady gaze at Max. A hint of a smile indicated he was either teasing his nephew or revealing a well-kept secret.

Max began to think of him as his Weird Uncle Bob about six months ago. This was right after Bob not only rid his house of the microwave oven after reading on the Internet that microwaves "killed living food," but he actually buried the nuker in the backyard to prevent others from being affected by its deadly technology. Bob seemed to get a lot of strange ideas from the Internet—at one point, he proclaimed aliens used the Web as a transportation device. Max laughed at that, thinking that his uncle could not believe such outrageousness, but now he wasn't sure. Bob also once said that he could email God. Max wondered if the aliens that traveled online ever visited God or if they just sent Him instant messages.

The "portals" of which Bob spoke were spots of random sizes that bespeckled photos taken on a beach with a digital camera. Bob had taken a trip to Galveston the previous weekend and now displayed the photos taken there on his laptop for his nephew to see.

A thought passed through Max's mind that maybe a particular video game influenced his weird uncle, but dismissed that idea because fifty-two-year-old Robert Gutermuth, an electrician who only discovered electronics the year before last, had never played a video game in his life. While the word "portals" conjured images in Max's mind of lightning-blue holes appearing to allow characters to move from one playing level to another, he was sure that to his uncle, it most likely meant clunky metal doors on a submarine.

"Uncle Bob," Max said, trying to sound patient and not condescending, "those are water droplets."

"No, they're not. If they were water droplets, they'd be the same in every picture because they'd leave a stain on the lens. But see..." He switched between one photo of still Gulf water nestled against flat sand and another identical picture. The only dissimilar elements were round imperfections of various sizes that dotted the screen. They differed with each shot. "They change. The portals move."

"Uncle Bob," Max said again. He almost said "Weird Uncle Bob" and had to pre-censor himself. "You aimed the camera at the beach. Water spray hit the lens and evaporated. More spray landed on the lens when you took the next picture. It's pretty obvious."

"The lens is too small." To prove his point, Bob pulled a small digital point-and-shoot camera out of his computer bag. He showed Max the tiny glass aperture on the device. "If water sprayed on it, it would cover the entire lens."

"Hmm," Max grunted. He didn't agree, but didn't want to argue the point.

"The portals can't be seen with the human eye. No one can tell they're there. But digital technology has changed that. This," he said, motioning to the camera, "is modern magic. With cameras like these, we can now see the invisible world around us."

Max didn't believe what his uncle said, but was curious about where this conversation was leading. With Weird Uncle Bob, you never knew, but it always ended somewhere interesting if not believable. "Where do the portals go?"

Bob looked around the living room. Even though the house was unusually quiet because of the rest of Max's family being elsewhere, Bob leaned in toward Max and whispered to the boy in a conspiratorial manner.

"The Earth has six major energy centers," he explained. "There's one in the Bermuda Triangle, another at the North Pole, and others spread around the globe. They provide the psychic power to everyone on Earth. Without these portals emitting their energy, life on the planet would cease."

"But where does the energy come from?"

A twinkle gleamed in Bob's eyes, the creases at the

corners deepening like a chiseled etching. "Like Rod Serling used to say, there is a fifth dimension. It's not of the physical plane, but a state of mind. The beings that exist there are of pure thought."

"No bodies?"

"No bodies."

Max let this sink in. He still didn't believe it; however, the gravity in Bob's voice, the surety in his body language, and the way his eyes seemed to say, *"This is for real,"* made Max want to believe. He was an adolescent Fox Mulder.

"How do people live without bodies?" Max suspected that Weird Uncle Bob was making this up as he went along, but he was curious what Bob's imagination would conjure. The dreamer part of himself pushed aside the skeptic in him.

"Because they're pure energy." Bob's voice remained in a strong whisper that made even the silliest of ideas interesting. "They exist all around us, but can only travel between our world and theirs through these."

His finger tapped the computer screen, pointing out one of the larger orbs that seemed to float over the beach.

"What if..." Max wasn't sure if he should continue the thought, but he found his courage. "What if one of us—a regular human, I mean—went through a portal?"

Bob grinned and sat back in his chair. "*That* is an excellent question."

LIFE CONTINUED, THE WAY IT HAS A BAD HABIT OF DOING. MAX returned to his ordinary regimen of that of a middle schooler. The ritual of morning prep, attending class, avoiding homework until the last minute, texting with friends, and squeezing in as many hours of entertainment that a day allowed filled Max's waking moments.

Weird Uncle Bob went back to his life, and Max's thoughts of him disappeared to the recesses of his mind. As was often the case with family and friends, love doesn't diminish, but when they were elsewhere, they were simply low on the thought order.

So it was with Max regarding Uncle Bob. Now and then (in particular when Max played a particular video game), the idea of portals and energy beings crossed his mind. He gave this concept a cursory pondering and then proceeded to more important issues in the life of a young teen.

Three weeks after Bob's visit, Max wandered into the kitchen to dig into the refrigerator. He had already eaten dinner and one snack, yet was craving more. If only there were energy portals for teenagers...

"No, I haven't talked to him in a couple of weeks," Max's mom said into her cell phone. She was cleaning up the dinner dishes with one hand while the other held the wireless device to her ear. She circled around Max like mothers learn to do when their children are underfoot.

Max tuned her out, like children often do when their mothers are engaged in a conversation that doesn't apply to them. He found a bowl of tuna fish that had been in the fridge for three days. He considered the pros and cons of slapping it on some bread and eating it as a sandwich or just spooning it out of the bowl.

"What do you mean, missing?" Kimberly Gardner's tone and demeanor changed abruptly, catching Max's attention. His mother froze in place, her back becoming rigid. Her free hand drifted to her face with the index finger tracing the ridge of her lower lip. Creases of concern furrowed her forehead.

Max regarded her with curiosity. This bit of mystery was more interesting than tuna fish.

"That's crazy. He wouldn't just take off without telling someone."

He? Max made a mental checklist of all the males to which his mother might be referring.

"Yes, I know he has strange ideas sometimes. That doesn't mean he's unstable."

Ah. Weird Uncle Bob. It made sense now. Whoever was on the other end of the phone knew Bob and his oddities, and also knew that Kimberly was his sister. For reasons unknown, Bob was nowhere to be found, so this unknown person contacted her out of distress or apprehension. Max's mother was not one to succumb to cries of alarm—she was grounded and sensible.

"Has anyone checked inside his house to make sure he didn't have an accident?" She listened to the other person speak, her lips pursed together. "Has anyone called the police?"

Anxiety surged through Max's nervous system. If his mother was talking about police involvement, this must be serious.

"What happened to Uncle Bob?" he asked.

Kimberly shooed him away, trying to hear the voice on the phone. "Okay, look, Dave and I will run over there and check out his place. I'm sure there's a reasonable explanation for this."

After hanging up, Kimberly dragged her husband away from ESPN to give him the news. Max insisted on being present, having already heard her half of the telephone conversation, and he wanted to be filled in on the rest. His parents allowed him to stay, but felt it best not to include his younger sister Maddy, who was only ten and would be too distressed by this. Bad news always upset her.

Kimberly explained that the person who called was a guy named John McAllister. John worked with Bob and had known Kimberly through a walk-a-thon that both of them took part in every year. He had informed her that Bob had not gone into work for several days and there was no answer when his employer tried to call him. None of Bob's and John's mutual friends knew where he was, either. Neighbors had last seen him over the weekend when he had driven away. The car wasn't in the driveway and the house remained dark, so apparently he had not returned home.

Max knew that since Bob had divorced nine years ago, his uncle had taken an active part in many community activities and several recently discovered on-line groups that his uncle said were composed of "like-minded individuals."

Kimberly ranted about those groups. "They're weirdos with no grasp on reality. Who can tell what people like that are capable of? The police need to investigate them."

"I'm sure if it comes to it, the police will do everything possible to find him." Dave sounded like the voice of reason, but Max recognized the tone as one meant to placate his mother when she became excited.

"He always falls for every harebrained idea that comes along," she continued, as if Dave had not spoken. Max heard this routine many times and understood that Bob believed whole-heartily in some wacky notion until exposed to another, even more ludicrous one. Max found it endearing. To his mother, it was exasperating.

Kimberly and Dave went to Bob's house, leaving Max behind to stay with Maddy, much to his consternation. He could do nothing about it, though, so he stayed in his room and sulked. Even *World of Warcraft* wasn't enjoyable to him.

His parents found nothing out of the ordinary. The laptop was gone, but that wasn't surprising since Bob tended to take it everywhere he went. By all appearances, he left the house and simply never returned. Where he went and why he didn't come back was anyone's guess. The only thing left was to contact the police.

The next day, Bob's car turned up. It had been impounded after sitting parked at a beach in Galveston for several days. Kimberly and Dave got it out of the impound, using the spare key Bob had left with her. Miraculously, they found the laptop in the car, but the cheapie digital camera was gone. It seemed Bob had the camera with him when he vanished.

Vanished. That word bounced around inside Max's skull. Bob had seemingly dropped off the face of the Earth. Police found no records of him in any hospital or morgue. If he drowned in the ocean, his body would have washed ashore by now. Max didn't think Bob was dead. He considered what Bob had told him regarding the portal and Max's own question about a person going through it.

No, that was all crazy talk. It was Weird Uncle Bob talk.

There's no way Bob actually believed what he said. It was conjecture by a man with an overactive imagination entertaining a kid with a similarly imaginative mind.

Wasn't it?

No portals existed. No fifth dimension. *The Twilight Zone* was just a TV show; the outlandish things that happened in those stories did not exist in real life. Inter-dimensional energy beings were fun to think about as a hypothetical, but only mentally unstable people thought they truly existed.

The problem was, Max couldn't convince himself of this. Unless the mafia kidnapped his uncle off the beach, what other explanation was there?

Max visualized Bob standing on the sand with the waves rolling up toward him, almost but not quite touching his loafers before retreating into the Gulf. Bob had his camera in his hand, snapping photo after photo, the ocean spray hitting him in the face, yet the droplets not quite penetrating the opening around the camera's lens. The LCD monitor displayed the shoreline in its pixels; but also present, barely perceptible, were round orbs that were *not* drops of water drying on the glass.

Lying on his bed with posters of Boba Fett and Arwen gazing down upon him, Max stared at the ceiling made of that popcorn stuff that snowed down on you if anything like a stray Nerf ball hit it. Little round white balls of various diameters spread out from wall to wall. He wondered if there were any portals hidden among those plaster globules. That's definitely something Max could appreciate—popcorn energy.

An idea struck him. If he took a picture of the ceiling popcorn, would the portals appear? He found his own camera, which was no more expensive than his uncle's. Aiming the camera straight up, he fired off three shots. The flashlight bursts temporarily blinded him. He blinked repeatedly to regain his vision.

Max viewed the pictures he just took on the camera's small screen, but all he could see was what looked like a mass of washed-out pimples. His eyes still must have been acting funky because something else was there—some faint shape, almost like a face.

No, that was just eye strain from looking at a poor-quality readout in dim lighting. Or the camera was just screwing up. After all, he didn't treat it as a sensitive piece of electronics, but a toy that could be tossed around as he pleased. The odd thing was, the strange ghost-image was different in every photo.

He went to the living room computer. His parents refused to allow him to have his own PC, and he couldn't comprehend why they didn't trust him to have one in his bedroom—it was just another unfair rule parents enforced on kids with no good rationale. Adults just like to torment those younger than them, that's all.

Max slipped the camera's memory card into the computer's card reader slot and then pulled up the pictures.

He let out an audible gasp that surprised him. Normally, he would have laughed at the sound he made. But not now. Unreality washed over Max. His stomach clenched. He felt faint. He grasped the keyboard, as if that would prevent him from falling to the floor.

On the computer monitor, Bob stared at him.

Bob's image was faintly superimposed over that of the

popcorn ceiling. Only half of his face was visible—the rest dissolved into the irregular moonscape surface.

The next photo showed something similar, though Bob's image had changed somewhat. The perspective was different, as was his expression. What was he trying to convey? If only the image were clearer.

In the last picture, Bob was closer to the camera. Max discerned Bob's left eye and most of his mouth, which was shaped like an O, as if he was trying to say something. What was it?

Was that fear showing on Bob's face? Excitement? Anguish? Joy? It was too hard to tell.

Max enlarged each photo and examined the details more closely. It didn't help, as all that did was distort the likeness into a jigsaw orchestration of colored squares that lost meaning.

One thing was certain, though—Bob had entered another dimension while at the beach in Galveston and was now trying to communicate with Max.

It looked like he was speaking. Of course, still photographs couldn't capture sound.

Max snorted a laugh as realization overcame him.

Video could.

He retrieved the memory card, slammed it back in the camera, and then dashed into his room.

"Don't run through the house!" his mother's voice trailed after the door slammed behind him. He launched himself across the room and bounced to a landing on his bed.

His fingers nimbly adjusted the camera's settings to record the video. He aimed the device back toward the ceiling again, hoping his meager lamp gave off enough light for recording. He held it as steady as he could for a while; the seconds lasting an eternity each.

When he couldn't take it anymore, Max ended the recording. He pressed the playback button, but the camera had to process the media. The progress bar showing on the display took great pleasure in torturing him. It ran to almost, but not quite, the end and then stopped. It sat there for an endless amount of time. Max was familiar with the phrase "pregnant pause," but this was carrying the entire population of the planet to term.

Finally, the video played.

"Max," Bob's voice said, sounding tiny and tinny from the minuscule speaker on the side of the camera. Max squashed it against his ear. He didn't notice the tears streaming out of his eyes.

"You have no idea what it's like," Bob's apparition continued. His voice had an odd quality to it, like he was a stroke victim learning to talk all over again. It was Bob, but not quite. "I suppose this is the closest to being dead without actually dying. It's unlike anything you can ever experience on Earth. I wanted to t—"

The video ended.

"No!" Max yelled, shaking the camera.

Coming to his senses, Max made another recording, this time longer.

"I'm so glad I could share this with you, Max," said Bob over the camera's playback. "Nobody ever believed me when I told them things. They didn't have the higher under-standing that I did, so that made me sound crazy. But you knew better. You're the only one. We have that special connection, you and I. That's why I was able to come to you. Your energy drew me. Now I can share my wondrous discovery with you. If only you could see and feel what I can. The human body is so limited, so blunt. We waste so much energy and take for gra—"

That video clip reached its end.

"How'd you do it, Bob?" Max asked the air. "How'd you get through the portal?"

He recorded again, counting to ten. That should be enough time for Bob to answer his question, Max thought.

"I didn't think I could, not at first," Bob answered. "I called out to them, reached out with my mind and all my energy. The port—"

"Ugh!" Max exclaimed. Obviously, it wasn't enough time. Bob could be long-winded and not get to the point immediately. "Sorry, it cut you off. Can you repeat what you were saying?"

The next recording: "Somehow my energy formed a psychic connection with that of the portals. I could feel them all around me. It was a tingling, electric sensation that wasn't unpleasant, but was unearthly.

"As I took more and more photos, the portals grew larger. I think they were merging, smaller ones into a much bigger one, like bubbles joining together. At some point, what I considered the grand portal became somewhat visible to me, like an object just outside my peripheral vision, only right in front of me. Then it enveloped me.

"It was warm, but not on my skin. The warmth penetrated my entire essence. I felt purified, as if my soul were cleansed. It was perfect comfort, unadulterated relaxation. I gave myself to the portal."

"What's it like there?" Max asked, his excitement level at a fever pitch. "Can you see the energy beings? What are they like? Can you eat?"

"It's hard to say what the other dimension is like," Bob replied. "How do you explain color to a blind man? Yes, I sense the presence of the beings. Since technically I'm composed of energy in this realm, I'm not really seeing or hearing in the traditional sense. It's an awareness. I'm like a child to them, just learning to crawl and make sounds, so communication is primitive. Since I have no physical body, my nourishment is the replenishing of energy."

"Can you see me? How can you make sounds?"

"I'm aware of your presence. Your energy draws me to you. I was right in the fact that digital technology was the key to bridging the gap between the physical plane and the one I now inhabit. I can manifest radiation of specific wavelengths that can be read by electronic instruments. Those are interpreted as light and sound."

"This is so awesome," Max said, grinning so broadly as to be painful.

He raced out of his room, calling for his parents.

"What is all the commotion?" Kimberly asked. Her brother's disappearance had taken its toll on her, and she was not in the mood for foolishness.

"You gotta see this!" Max yelled. He slid the memory card into the computer. "Dad, come here, quick!"

His father sauntered to the computer wearing an exasperated expression.

Max pulled up the third photo, since that had captured Bob's likeness the best. He waited with exuberance for the reaction from his parents.

"What are we looking at?" Dave asked.

Max was confused, but figured it was like one of those magic eye paintings where the hidden image became obvious only when you adjusted the way you perceived it. He traced Bob's outline. "Look, right here."

Kimberly and Dave exchanged a glance and shrugged.

"It's Uncle Bob!" Max said, losing his patience.

"Oh, for heaven's sake," Kimberly said and turned to walk away.

"You don't see him?" Max asked, perplexed. "He's right there."

"Max, this isn't funny," said Dave.

"I'm not trying to be funny. Here, listen to this."

He played the first video.

"What are we supposed to be hearing?" his father asked. "All I hear is static."

"What? I recorded Uncle Bob talking to me in my room. It's playing right now! You don't hear it?"

Uncharacteristic of Kimberly, she burst into tears and fled.

"Is this your idea of a practical joke?" Dave growled at his son. "Are you intentionally trying to hurt your mother?"

"No, Dad—"

It was too late. Dave followed Kimberly to their room, leaving Max alone at the computer.

Well, not quite alone.

"Nice going, stupid," Maddy said, peering around the corner. She could always be counted on for moral support.

Max returned to his bedroom, not trying to hide the fact that he, too, was now crying.

"What's going on?" he pleaded to his invisible uncle. "Why can't they see and hear you?"

He recorded silence, and silence is all that played back. Bob was no longer with him—if he had been there at all.

THE POLICE FOUND NO FURTHER LEADS TO BOB'S DISAPPEARANCE. Bob's credit cards and bank account had not been used. His cell phone had no activity. There were no sightings of a person matching his description in Galveston. The police figured he was undergoing a midlife crisis and dropped out of communication with everyone. They assumed he parked his car at the beach and hitched a ride to some other part of the country. Eventually, he would turn up. With that outlook, the investigation ended.

Kimberly knew the police were wrong and said as much multiple times. She was vocal about her opinions of the police as well, though eventually she let both topics go silent. As the weeks passed, she withdrew into herself. She was less talkative, did not smile or laugh, and only performed her responsibilities around the home perfunctorily, with a lack of enthusiasm.

Max thought of her as a pod person—there in body, but not in spirit. This was the opposite of his uncle, who was in spirit but not body.

The boy never brought up his visitations from Bob with his parents again. Max knew they would not believe him and it would just cause more problems if he pushed the issue. Behind his closed door, he continued reaching out to

Bob, talking to him and hoping for a response. The camera captured no image and no audio from Bob; if the man or whatever he had become was there, he wasn't making himself known.

Max couldn't figure out why he was the only one who could see and hear Bob on the recordings. He narrowed it down to two possibilities: somehow Bob tapped into Max's energy pattern so that only Max could discern those particular wavelengths; or Max was crazy. He accepted either answer.

He played the recordings over and over while alone, trying to discern some clues about how to communicate once again with Bob. He wanted proof to show to his parents, hoping his mother would accept the fact that her brother was now living in another dimension. The video and audio were the same every time he played the files, so if he was experiencing hallucinations, his brain did a good job repeating them verbatim.

The portals were the key. Somehow, Bob had traveled through the portals from the other dimension to communicate with Max. Perhaps that was a temporary visit and Bob could not repeat it.

Maybe he was not allowed to return.

What exactly were those energy beings? Bob never explained that. Were they the spirits of dead people? Aliens? Angels? Ancient entities that have always been on Earth but existing on a different plane? Did they have knowledge of humans before now? Was Bob the first human to contact them? What did they think of us? Were we a threat to them?

The question that looped in Max's mind most often was whether Bob remained in the other dimension of his own accord. His physical body may have been destroyed, which meant he could never come back to this plane. Or maybe the energy beings were keeping him there against his will.

Max had seen enough science fiction movies to know what people expected first contact with intelligent non-human creatures would be like. Usually, violence ensued, either from humans attacking the aliens out of ignorance or the aliens wanting to wipe out the humans. While there were a few movies that showed peaceful co-existence, Max thought that was unlikely to happen in real life.

If the government discovered the portals, would the officials destroy them? Could the portals be destroyed?

Intuition told Max if he was going to find any answers, he would have to go to the source. Upon contemplation, he figured out how to do this. He tracked down his father.

"I'm worried about Mom," he told his dad. "Ever since Uncle Bob disappeared, she hasn't been herself."

"She's been very upset about the whole thing," Dave said, trying to watch CNN around his son.

"Yeah, I was thinking about that. Maybe what she needs is some sort of memorial for him. You know, for closure."

"We don't know that he's dead."

"That's what Mom thinks."

Dave shrugged.

"If we go to the place where he went missing, we could say a few words about him, put some flowers down—you know, honor him." Max said.

"You just want to go to the beach," his dad replied.

"It wouldn't hurt for us to get out of the house," Max reasoned. "It might break the tension around here."

Dave sighed. "I'll think about it."

Not only did he think about it, but Dave discussed it with his wife. Kimberly rejected the idea at first, but then thought they might find something the police missed. And she too realized that the family could use a break.

The following Saturday, the Gardner family drove to Galveston, parking in the lot where Bob's car was found. Kimberly was not one for sentimental ceremony, but she did as Max advised and brought a simple bouquet that she placed in the surf. Afterward, she and Dave strolled hand-in-hand along the beach while Maddy ran in and out of the water.

Once his family was far from him, Max took out the camera and snapped a few shots of the beach and the Gulf. He checked out the results, and sure enough, he saw random spots on the photos that changed from one shot to another.

"Okay, Uncle Bob," he called out to the air. "I'm here. What now?"

He recorded a half a minute of video, and then played it back with the camera's speaker pressed against his ear. The only sound on the playback was the whirl of the wind.

Max spent the next half an hour taking various pictures and recording video. Nothing else happened with the portals, if they even existed. He was on the verge of giving up and joining his parents and sister when it happened.

It started with a tingling sensation on his skin that made the fine hair on his arms stand on end. Max's vision clouded over, but he soon realized that it wasn't his eyes that were the problem; the haze in his vision was a circular obfuscation floating in the air before him. Beyond it, he could see his family walking toward him, though their forms were indistinct, like an expressionist painting. Their lackadaisical attitude told him they did not notice the portal, which grew with every second.

As the portal encompassed him, a peaceful feeling unlike anything Max had ever felt before flowed through him. It was like every muscle in his body unknotted at once. Somehow he stayed standing, even though he felt as if he were melting into a fluid, non-corporeal pool.

The world around him—his world, the normal world—became opaque. A barrier rapidly solidified, separating him from the normal plane of existence. Max wondered how he looked to his family, whether he was standing on the beach as if nothing was happening to him, or if he was fading from existence.

Like a cracking egg, a seam of light streamed out before him. It was so bright it should have blinded him, but his eyes did not hurt by gazing into it. The light enveloped him.

Max was now in a dream state, simultaneously real and not real. His mind was sharp, more than at any time in his life. However, he could no longer sense his body, as if he were composed solely of thought.

Time no longer existed. In many respects, *Max* no longer existed. He did not care.

At some point, he realized Bob was with him. He could not see his uncle, for his eyes were not working. Instead, Max sensed him, like their minds were linked.

"Am I dead?" Max asked without speaking.

"No," Bob answered. Max didn't hear Bob's voice, but the message appeared in his mind as a complete thought.

"Have I gone through the portal?"

"Not yet. You're in transition. I met you here before you

completely crossed over. Once that happens, your body will be converted to energy. There's no going back."

"I want to be with you. I want to be like you."

"I can't stop you," Bob said. "But if you continue on, you will never see your family or friends again. You won't finish growing up because you'll no longer be human. Your whole existence will be different."

"But I need to know what it's like!" Max exclaimed. He could not communicate his desperate need for knowledge with words, but somehow he transmitted the idea.

Bob understood. Through this new brain link, Max sensed that his uncle felt the same thing, only more intensely. Bob had sought answers his whole life; he quested for information about the universe, about God, about the very fabric of existence. He moved from one ideology to another, piecing together his own ideas of what made life the way it was, but nothing quite satisfied his longing. Something was always missing.

Once Bob traveled through the portal, that all changed. His understanding clarified. He was like a child again, exposed to a new world. However, the answers he received only created more questions. He had so much to learn, and his journey to knowledge had just started.

However, it came at a cost. He had to give up everything —his family, his body, his humanity. The only reason he could contact Max soon after crossing over was because of their strong bond, but he would not be able to repeat it.

If Max followed his uncle, he would have to do the same by giving up everything. This was Bob's lifelong desire; it wasn't Max's. The magnitude of the situation sunk in with perfect lucidity.

"The portals will always be there," Bob said. This was an individual statement projected into Max's mind rather than the instant communication they had been sharing. Their link was breaking.

"I hope you find what you're looking for," Max said.

Bob's goodbye was not thought, but emotion. It was more complicated than love, but Max could not decipher all its nuances. Yet he understood.

The sun glared off the sand.

Max blinked. He rubbed his eyes. The fugue passed.

"Max, are you okay?" Kimberly asked. She, Dave, and Maddy stood next to him, looking concerned.

"Just zoning out, that's all," Max said, flashing them a genuine grin. "Thinking about Uncle Bob."

"Yeah, me too," she said.

"He's okay, Mom. He really is."

"I know."

Max's mother hugged him. Nothing else in the world mattered.

POSTHUMOUS

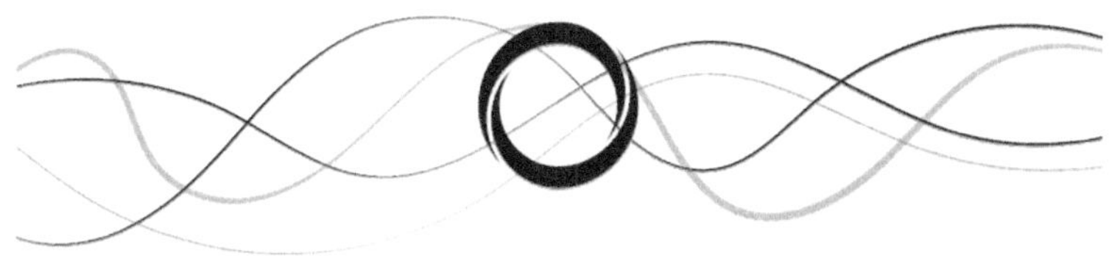

Consciousness returned at the speed of melted water dripping off a glacier. At some point, he realized he was aware of his hazy surroundings, as if gauze covered his eyes and plugs filled his ears. The surroundings were indistinct shapes set in a gray gloom, providing no sign of his actual location.

He tried to dredge up some memory of his life before the condition—he was suffering from some condition, though he could not think of what it was. It obviously caused his current confusion and fugue.

His brain functioned at an excruciatingly slow pace. Forgotten fragments of his past floated through his mind, but they were unconnected, incoherent images rather than anything substantial. A sunset. A dog barking. A pair of shoes. A phone. A woman's laugh.

Sam? No, that name wasn't quite right. Maybe Stan. Yes, that sounded more accurate. The longer he let the name simmer in his struggling thoughts, the more he became convinced that Stan was his name. Beyond that, emptiness.

Stan forced his legs to move. The appendages did not want to function, but the stiff muscles conceded and allowed him to stagger forward several steps. His joints screamed out in protest, surging a sensation quite unlike pain through his body—in fact, his nerves were deadened, beyond acknowledging his own existence.

Where was he to go? He felt the need to move, despite his body deciding otherwise. If he knew where home was, he would head there. Of course, he didn't even know where *he* was, though he thought other people might be nearby just out of his limited sight. The ghost of the sound of someone, or perhaps *someones*, hovered at the precipice of actual recognition.

Another name drifted to him like a phantom in the dark. Allison. The name provided the comfort of familiarity without the benefit of knowing the person attached to it. Powerful emotion battered the wall of sensory deprivation that imprisoned him. Another word latched onto her name, binding to it like a chemical reaction—wife. Except that wasn't completely accurate. *Ex-wife.*

As if it were instinct embedded in his genetic makeup, Stan understood he had once been married to this Allison person, but that marriage had ended some time ago. Children? No, they had none. There had been love, and loss, and loneliness related to her, but those emotions were now merely echoes reverberating in the vast, vacant recesses of his soul.

He bumped into something and realized that it was another person. Was he supposed to say something? He knew there was a phrase appropriate in a situation like this, but it was out of his grasp. He moved his mouth, expecting that whatever he could not remember would be spoken, but his jaw moved, vocalizing nothing more than a guttural groan. The other person did not respond, but shuffled away into that murky miasma.

Allison. Allison. Allison. Stan ran the name through his mind, hoping it would trigger more memories. A house—not large, but sufficient. The small yard had green sod. The neighborhood was pleasant, middle-class. Wait, that house belonged to the past, in his life before the divorce. It was one of the many things he lost with that trauma.

Losing his wife, along with a good portion of his life, stirred as strong of a reaction in Stan's recessed psyche as the love for her did. He remembered the overwhelming pain, the grief, the sense of helplessness and futility, but it was nothing but memory—the emotion itself did not surface, and neither did the love he knew had been ever present. His new condition not only ravaged his body but also the essence of what made him a person. He noted this with a disconnected observance, like a horse would to a bird flying through its pasture—noticing its presence but unaffected by it, and promptly forgetting the bird when it flies away.

Stan's leg buckled, and he aimed his eyes downward to see that he had stepped off a concrete curb. He found himself in the middle of a street. His senses acclimatized to his new state—they were still present, but the information from his nerve endings to his brain was stunted and took longer to process. The world around him sharpened into focus, like images in old Polaroid photos gradually appearing on the paper.

Tall buildings walled him in on two sides. He knew this place, or at least thought he did. An odd sense that he had spent a lot of time in this city block filled him. It was quite reassuring. More snippets of his past surged into his lumbering mind—an office, a computer, piles of papers. The corpse of negative sentiment toward his occupation visited him just long enough for Stan to notice before it wandered into obscurity. *Insurance agent.* Stan hated the job, but it paid the bills. That was a long time ago, before *now*. He would never go into that dreaded agency again.

Others surrounded him. They all had Stan's condition. This wasn't a fully formed thought in Stan's brain, but an inherent understanding, like insects of the same species recognizing one another. These other people were in various stages, and Stan realized he was much better off. He could discern nothing terribly out of the ordinary about his body other than the awkwardness and rigidity of his movements. Some people in the street with him were missing parts of their bodies. One dragged himself along the pavement with his hands, as his legs were gone. They ambled in random directions with no purpose. Uncomprehending, Stan joined in as one of the herd just the same.

A woman stopped. Her head snapped up faster than Stan thought was possible under the circumstances. Her attention focused on the far side of the street. She lurched forward in that direction. Two others gravitated that way as well. Others followed.

Then Stan's senses energized. The smell was electric, more vivid than any of the apparitions that passed themselves off as memories. He felt compelled to go toward the source of this wondrous aroma. It overtook him, and if he had any control before, it fled and left him vulnerable to this compulsion.

His body worked on its own accord, pushing him closer and closer to its target. The other victims of whatever medical crisis he was experiencing crowded together. The urgency thickened around them. It became unbearable to Stan. His hands groped out before him, pushing past those who were slow and feeble.

Movement ahead, like a panicked rabbit.

The intensity crushed Stan until he felt he would explode.

A noise. A terrible high-pitched noise. A wonderful, vigorous noise.

His fingers latched onto his prize. The death grip would never release. Like claws, they tore and ripped, bringing to his mouth the joyous reward.

Flesh.

Warm, delicious blood flowed.

It wasn't Stan's stomach that commanded him, but rather a more primitive force that barricaded every thought, feeling, and sensation except for one craving—the need to feed.

As his irresistible passion was being satisfied, one delicacy that trumped all else thrust its glorious presence into Stan's awareness. His solitary, uncompromising goal was to consume it.

Gray matter.

A CLEAR AND CALM NIGHT
A TALE OF TERROR

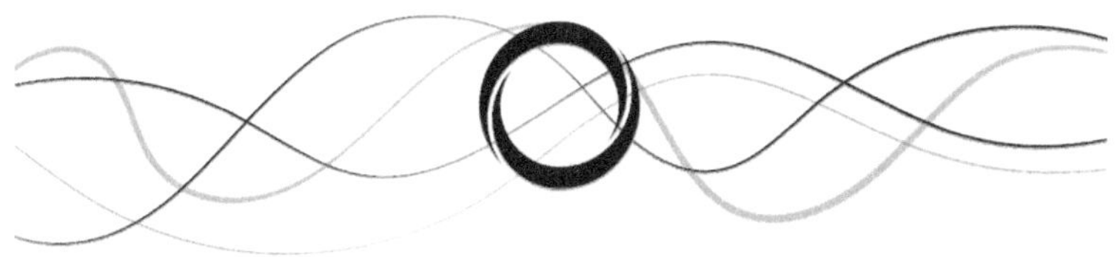

Horror stories seem to thrive on the old cliché that they take place on dark and stormy nights. However, the most terrifying experience of my life happened in the wee hours of a spring day when the full moon shone so brightly that it was practically daylight, with a pleasant calmness permeating the air.

I was a perpetual college student, taking a couple of classes each semester just to keep my enrollment status, so I didn't have to begin the tortuous process of paying back student loans. By the time I was 26, I had finally earned enough credits to be classified as a senior under the auspicious major of Liberal Arts, my third such degree program. I considered changing to International Relations, though Food Science was not out of the question; I certainly would never be a molecular biologist.

On the night in question, I had gotten off work from my

current job as a clerk at a local convenience store called E-Z-Stor, a dingy little mom-and-pop establishment with blinding overhead lights that revealed peeling tile floors and disheveled shelves stocked with mostly off-brand goods. Of course, I couldn't get out until twenty minutes after my shift ended because the lazy bum who worked the third shift was late yet again.

"Thanks for covering for me, man," the kid with the stringy hair (was his name Greg or Craig?) said after strolling into the store without an apparent care in the world. "I owe you one." He owed me more than one. Unfortunately, he could never pay up.

The E-Z-Stor was the last place to get gas or munchies on the outskirts of town and sat on a corner where a traffic light had recently replaced a yellow blinker. Flat farm land surrounded the store. In the years since, subdivisions replaced the fields of corn and soybeans, and the E-Z-Stor became a Walmart.

I stepped out into the fresh air devoid of automobile fumes, clearing my sinuses clogged from the bleach I used on the indoor floor. Being a night owl, I was most alive after midnight. Various friends and family members often referred to me as a vampire or a werewolf, but I was only a zombie when I had to wake early in the morning. On this night, I was fully human and had no desire to return home so soon.

The moon compelled me. Yes, I know that sounds silly while sitting there in your comfortable chair under the soft glow of your lamp, presumably with enjoyable music playing in the background. There's really no other way to describe it. The white orb looking down at me from a cloudless sky surrounded by millions of twinkling stars appeared larger than normal. It was so clear the "face" made by lunar craters stood out in stark relief in the sunlight reflecting off its surface. It's easy to understand how ancient man believed that the moon was magical while peering up, mouths gaping, at this mysterious glowing object that waxed and waned every month. It was now at full wax.

Maybe I was part werewolf after all, since the urge to commune with nature beckoned me with lupine strength. Usually the nearby fields, which had yet to be cultivated for the new growing season, were just background noise to me —ever present and non-changing, with little stimulation for the senses. Tonight, they were uncharted territory, calling out for an explorer to venture into their wilds.

The parking lot wrapped around the building with the dumpster hidden at the rear. A two-foot cement wall separated the pavement with the corn field directly behind the store. I bound up onto the wall and perched there like a cat waiting to pounce on an unsuspecting grasshopper. Like a little kid on a playground, I leaped onto the waiting dirt and ran into the remains of the dry cornstalks that survived the winter. The world took on a high-contrast blue-and-white façade in the moonlight; the stalks silhouetted tentacles reaching out of the ground like the claws of a buried monstrosity.

A slight cool breeze pushed the hair back from my face. I was a nocturnal gazelle, loping through the acres of desolate terrain. Eventually, exhaustion grabbed hold of me, and I stopped to catch my breath, hands on my knees, heart pounding in my ears. I was alive and free and exhilarated. Sure, I was an uncommitted student with a growing mountain of debt working a crappy job—and the less said about my love life, the better—but at that moment, I felt transported to a higher realm. I had left Earth and was journeying through the galaxy like an unguided spirit floating freely to an unknown world. Life was flawless.

The media loves to destroy heroes—a popular person will inevitably be denigrated and the masses who used to be fans will turn against them. The Universe apparently adopts this technique also—as soon as you feel that you've made it to the top, a landslide will bring you back down to the bottom so you have to climb back up again. I can imagine what Sisyphus felt like, repeatedly having to shove that boulder up the mountain in a never-ending futile struggle. In my naïveté, I assumed this euphoria I was experiencing would be eternal, or at least last until I could return home. However, it ended all too abruptly.

At first, it was just a series of inexplicable, unconnected events. A flock of birds roosting in the decaying stalks took flight with a flurry of wings that startled me from my out-of-body experience. I can't tell you what birds they were; they were just black shapes erupting from the surrounding field that quickly disappeared into the night sky.

Before I could force my stomach back down my throat, a cat yowled from somewhere nearby. It was an unholy sound that ripped through my very essence, not dissimilar to the wail of an off-tune saxophone played with a split reed. The feline shriek reached an aneurism-inducing pitch that caused me to claw at my ears. Then it stopped. I have no idea what fate the cat endured, but at least my misery—if not the cat's—ended.

A moment of absolute stillness fell over the field, then a

ripple moved through the corn, as if the stalks were doing the wave at a ball game. Air remained motionless; the plants themselves moved ostensibly of their own volition in a rehearsed pattern. The swell approached me and then passed by, taking no notice of me, only to fade away into the distant darkness. I didn't know what caused it, or even where it began, and I didn't care. I still don't care.

It was time for me to leave. I no longer felt like the world was perfect—in fact, an unsettling uneasiness crawled through my veins, spreading through all my extremities. I realized I was holding my breath, so I gasped an inhalation.

When I was little, my neighbors had a huge, gnarled oak in their front yard. By day, it was a great climbing tree where my friends and I spent hours of enjoyment dangling from its branches. However, if I remained outside after the sun went down, the previous plaything became an entity out of a nightmare I would run past in terror to make it back to the safety of my home. My rational mind knew it was the same tree, but my irrational subconscious took control and told me otherwise. *That evil thing's branches will surely reach out and grab you,* my inner self told me. *It will catch you and gobble you up. It will tear your arms and legs off. It will rip your flesh to pieces. It will—*

You get the idea.

You'd think that when a person passes the quarter century mark, those childish fears will evaporate like spittle on a summer day's sidewalk. If only that were true. On this night, which seemed so special but was quickly turning bizarre, my long forgotten nine-year-old self reared his ugly head. Gone was the terrifying tree, replaced with a barren landscape with no humanity in sight. I never felt so alone, so lost.

I turned back toward the E-Z-Stor, which was an overly-lit square on the dark horizon. How did it get so far away?

Moving in what felt like slow motion, I forced myself to walk; if I ran, I would panic. I didn't need customers—not to mention Greg-or-Craig—to see me racing into the parking lot in a frenzy. I reminded myself that I was getting worked up over nothing. Sure, just because birds that should have been sleeping all decided to take off all at the same time and a cat chose to scream for some unknown reason and the corn stalks wanted to perform a ballet routine didn't mean that I should have been frightened.

The reason I should have been frightened happened next.

Earthquakes were not unheard of in my part of the Midwest, but I had never experienced one—until now. I felt the rumble through my feet before I heard it. The ground trembled, a motion not too different from a people mover at an airport. It was enough to start my legs pumping. I didn't care what anyone might think of me charging out of the farmland in the dead of night; I had to get out of there.

The tremor intensified. My ankle twisted and nearly sent me sprawling, but I caught myself so that I only stumbled before picking up speed again. This was short-lived—the ground buckled in front of me, catapulting me head-first into the earth. The pungent smell of topsoil filled my nasal cavity as the actual topsoil filled my nostrils.

I rolled onto my back, snorting the dirt out of my nose. The field around me rose and fell like a turbulent ocean. I held on like I was in danger of falling off—where I'd fall to, I didn't want to know.

Okay, my adult mind said, taking tentative control from my child's mind, it's an earthquake. That's all. Just an earthquake. The animals could sense it first. The first minor blast moved the corn, but wasn't strong enough for me to feel it. Nothing supernatural. It'll pass soon. Just wait it out.

Time plays tricks when you're under stress, so it seemed much longer than it must have actually lasted. The earthquake eventually slowed and stopped, though my body could still feel the violence. Aftershocks were likely, so I wanted to get back to the store before one hit. The challenge was to engage my body when it was still suffering its own shock.

Panting heavily, I got to my knees and stood on all fours for a moment, psyching myself for the next step, the standing position. Before I could rise, the ground before me exploded. I threw an arm over my eyes to protect them from the flying debris and fell onto my back. That is probably what saved my life.

I'm not a very creative guy. I lack the attention span to spend on any projects that take imagination and innovation. My drawings look like scrawls from an infant. My knowledge of art stopped at whether a painting was a pretty picture. I couldn't make up a fictitious story if my mother's life depended on it. I'm not drawn to horror or fantasy movies; just give me a dumb action flick or a raunchy comedy and I'm happy. So believe me when I tell you I could no make this up. I just don't have that capability.

My eyes had not opened, yet I could feel the shadow fall over me. A sound that I imagine must be like that of a snake slithering through the grass amplified a thousand fold filled my ears. I resisted the urge to wipe the clumps of soil off my face and remained statue still. I cracked my eyelids.

A monstrosity emerged from a hole in the ground. Its torso was the breadth of a tractor tire. Multiple limbs radiated from its worm-like trunk. Its head faced away from me, displaying the profile of the largest beak I have ever seen. "Beak" was probably not the right word, but that's what it looked like. However, this was no bird. The creature ignored me and pulled itself the rest of the way out of the fissure. It rose to its full height of about twelve feet under two large legs at the base of its body that allowed it to walk upright. The bird-thing lumbered away from me and across the field.

The worst thing was the aroma. I once rode my bicycle past a meat processing plant, and the odor of slaughtered carcasses emanating from the concrete building was gag-inducing. I never passed that facility again. This was much more ghastly. It took all my effort to not vomit.

It's an awful feeling when your automatic bodily responses take over, whether it's hiccups or sneezes or something more personal and embarrassing. In my case, my nervous system chose that moment to throw me into convulsions. I spasmed on the ground uncontrollably and tried desperately to force it to stop while praying that whatever had just surfaced didn't notice me. I pictured a kitten ambushing a defenseless toy mouse twitching on the living room carpet.

I gained enough power over my treacherous body to sneak a peek in the direction the monstrosity headed. It was still traipsing on that bearing at a fast pace. Afraid that it might decide to make a return trip, I forced my arms and legs to operate and crawled. It didn't take long before adrenaline kicked in, and I rose to my feet and sprinted toward the store.

Thump! Thump!

Dread oozed from the top of my skull to my toes like saltwater poured into a container of fresh water. I glanced behind me to find my fear realized—the creature was in pursuit. Its gigantic frame swayed from side to side as it lumbered toward me on its impossibly long limbs. Somehow, I found another gear and bolted forward at an even faster speed.

THUMP!!! THUMP!!!

It was closing in. I could practically feel it breathing down my neck. Did it breathe?

I've heard people talk about terror blocking out all senses, but with me it was like I entered a hyper-reality. *Everything* stood out in clear detail. The crunch of my feet on the corn. The wheeze of my exchange of oxygen. A distant truck rumbling down the highway. The lights in the parking lot growing ever closer. The swarm of moths in the yellow glow of the incandescent bulbs. That distinctive moist springtime scent that promised recent growth. The foul reek of the unspeakable beast that must have been within a distance to snatch me off my feet.

It's interesting how random chance can sometimes change a person's life—the van that pulls out in front of a motorcyclist, the lottery numbers that match your ticket, the infectious person who sneezes right after you leave the building. My random chance had been a dog. It was just a mutt, one that probably wandered from one of the sprawling farms in the area. This dog was sniffing around the dumpster behind the E-Z-Stor when it saw an enormous shadow chasing a smaller shadow, heading the animal's way. Wanting to join in the fun, the dog scampered toward us, barking joyfully. I felt sorry for the little guy, I really did—but if it wasn't for him, I wouldn't be here today. He wasn't even acting heroically, but his presence caused enough of a distraction for me to slip over the cement wall to safety. I heard a yelp and caught just a glimpse of one stringy tentacle hauling him into the air. The beak clamped down on the pup.

CRUNCH!

I pressed myself length-wise against the short wall and hoped it was enough to hide me. I held my breath and willed my muscles to freeze. By the sound of it, the thing moved away, but not far. It may have been searching for me or just looking for a comfy place to finish its snack.

Get moving! I'm not sure if that was the adult mind or the child's mind speaking, but it was good advice. Edging forward on my side, I managed about a dozen feet before I thought it might be safe to make a dash to the side of the building. It was now or never, and I couldn't even chance one more look back. I really didn't want to know how close that thing was, anyway.

I jumped to my feet. Fire must have trailed behind me as I rounded the corner. In one second flat, I burst into the parking lot and zeroed in on my Honda, that had rolled out of the factory a decade earlier. Only one other car sat in the lot, the one that belonged to Greg-or-Craig. A moment of conscience overtook me; how could I not warn him of what I had just faced?

My sudden entrance startled him from his repose behind

the counter, causing him to spill the 44-ounce drink in his hand all over the car magazine that he surely picked up from the rack by the door.

He swore a none-too-original curse word at me. "What the hell are you doing here? I thought you left."

"Shut up and listen to me!"

Greg-or-Craig gawked at me, looking like a fish trying to breathe air.

"Don't go outside," I said, trying to sound reasonable even though I must have looked like a maniac. "Something just chased me through the field."

"What? A skunk?"

"No."

"Bobcat?"

"I don't know what it was. This mother was huge, though."

"A bear?"

"No! Just trust me. It ate a dog."

"Hot dog?"

"Stop being stupid and listen to me. We need to call the police."

"I gotta check this out." With a loopy grin on his face, Greg-or-Craig pushed past me and headed toward the door. I grabbed at him to stop him, but my fingers only snagged his shirt. He pushed me away with more force than I would have thought his scrawny frame was capable of. I suppose I wasn't in much of a condition to put up a fight. "Back off! What's your problem, anyway?"

Hmm, let's see. A subterranean monster just punched its way out of the Earth with the force of 4.2 on the Richter

Scale and gulped down someone's beloved pet instead of me. I wonder why I'm upset.

Thoughts are wonderful, but trying to vocalize them can be frustrating. Before I could get out the "hmm," Greg-or-Craig was out the door. Instead, I yelled, "Don't go!"

He made it two steps out into the open air when a shadow covered him. He turned his head upward, slack-jawed. A greenish gray appendage reached down and wrapped a long-fingered claw around him and lifted him out of sight. His screams penetrated the store's plate-glass window.

Crunch.

The window imploded as the lower half of my co-worker flew through the pane and landed with the legs draped over the candy display. I guess he didn't taste good. I reflected later that it was too bad that it wasn't his top half, because then I could have read his name badge.

With an amazing calm that must have been my entire system shutting down, I called 911 and said that someone was killed at the E-Z-Stor. I then went into the walk-in refrigerator, curled up in a ball on the floor, and passed out.

After some time, I realized I was looking at several police officers. I had been in a catatonic state and they took me to a hospital, but the cops waited until I returned to my senses in order to question me. I attempted to tell them the events of the evening, but it apparently came out as a jumbled mess.

Based on the blood splatters and the remains found, the police knew that whatever killed Greg-or-Craig was beyond my doing. My mutterings of a monster bursting from the cornfield were met with incredulity. I expect they must have searched the field, and if so, they had to have found the hole in the ground. What they did beyond that is anybody's guess. The only thing the local news reported was that a tragic accident happened, resulting in the death of a convenience store clerk.

Of course, I never returned to work at the E-Z-Stor.

I now live in Maine, the farthest point in the contiguous United States that I could move to. My nightmares eventually became less frequent, though they pop up now and then. Usually they're about the dog. One day I'll finish my Bachelor's degree.

Sometimes I think about going back to my hometown, and maybe I'll find the courage. I often wonder about those homes built where that corn field stood and the families that live in them—and what might burrow underneath them.

DARK

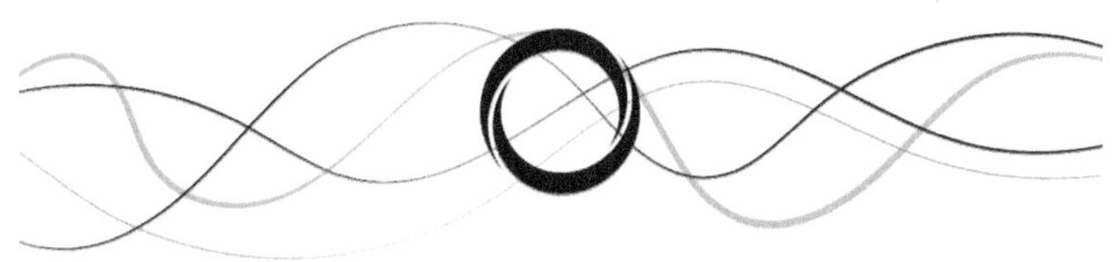

An unidentifiable noise woke me from a deep sleep, though when I opened my eyes, I saw nothing. It took me a few moments to realize that I was indeed awake.

Earlier, a vicious storm raged outside, but it had apparently abated, as I could not hear any wind or rain outside the window. However, cloud cover must have still blocked the moon and stars, as no light seeped in through the drawn blinds.

Usually the room was lit with faint light from various sources—the numbers on the alarm clock on the end table, the display of the DVD player, the red light on the HDTV. But none were now illuminated, leaving the room awash in pitch blackness. I assumed the storm knocked out the power in my house while I slept.

I felt around the table, looking for my smart phone. It had a flashlight app that was pretty bright. My hand fell upon the fake wood tabletop, came across some random papers and a half-filled glass of formerly iced tea that I nearly knocked over. No phone.

I sighed and wracked my brain, trying to remember where I had left it. When did I come to bed? I had been sitting in the living room watching Letterman and the satellite signal disappeared thanks to the hideous weather outside. I decided to lie down and read a while, and that's the last I remember. Sure enough, I found the paperback beside me on top of the blanket. Apparently, I had left my phone on the coffee table.

THUD!

The sound sent any fleeting sleep left in me scurrying away. I was now wide awake. What made that noise? Did it come from outside or inside the house? Was it my imagination?

I untangled my legs from the covers and swung them to the side of the bed. My mind raced—was I in danger? What could I use as a weapon? Who would find my body? I rose to my feet while my heart pounded in my throat and temples.

Fear clenched my stomach as I realized that my perfectly comfortable bedroom was now alien to me. I could not remember the layout of the room. Where was the door? How many steps from the bed was it? It was off to the left somewhere, but at what angle? If I just headed out in a direction using my best guess, I could easily plow into my dresser. I could see myself bashing my knee in the darkness, resulting in me crippling myself and allowing the prowler to prey upon me and stab or strangle me—

"Stop it!" I scolded myself. My voice was far too loud. I realized that the normal sounds of the house, like the air conditioning and the refrigerator, no longer filled the air with their low roars. This dark space I found myself in was dead, both in sight and in sound. That meant that my voice probably carried down the hall and to whoever lay in wait to kill me—

I punched my thigh to snap myself out of that thought. Nobody had broken into the house and was waiting to do me harm. That was just my over-tired brain jumping to a worst-case scenario thanks to the loss of power. All I had to do was find my phone and then I could see again. Then I'd locate a butcher knife.

My hands reached out into the abyss like those of the blind man that I essentially was and again contacted my night stand. I felt around until I found the wall, then made my way down the perimeter of the room. Finally, I reached the doorway and exited into the hallway.

My bare feet cautiously stepped onto the shallow carpet. I'm not in a habit of leaving things on the floor, but I'll inevitably step on the one thing that was mistakenly left lying there. Instead of stepping on some lost trinket, my foot landed in a wet spot.

Confused, I ran scenarios through my head, trying to figure out how my hall floor could have gotten soaked.

Maybe the ceiling leaked and the rain dripped in, causing this puddle. If there had been a leak, it had stopped because nothing dripped from above. I reached down and felt the moist carpet. The wetness formed an oblong shape a couple of inches wide and several more long—like the shape of a foot.

I dropped to my hands and knees and progressed down the corridor, patting the carpet in front of me. Sure enough, there was another wet spot of a similar shape. And another. A trail of these water-logged tracks led into the living room. Or away from it. I had no way of knowing which direction the person—or thing—that left these behind had gone.

The air in the house had suddenly become chilly. Goose bumps rose out of my flesh.

Was that breathing I heard? Or just a whoosh of wind through some undiscovered crack in the house's foundation?

I lived alone. After my bitter divorce, I swore I'd never remarry and so far I've kept that promise. I couldn't even bear to get another dog after my ex took my beloved Golden Retriever. But now, I realized how utterly alone I really was. If I were to die tonight, who would grieve for me?

My speed quickened as I tramped into the living room on all fours and smashed headfirst into the coffee table. Surely, whoever was in the house heard that and knew where I was. Perhaps he was standing only a few feet away, waiting to see what I was going to do. Waiting to make his move.

My hands scrambled over the table's glass top. They located a plastic rectangular device—the TV's remote control. I dropped it, not caring if it smashed the glass. My fingers grasped another object whose shape they knew so well—my phone. My thumb instinctively found the home button that activated the operating system, waking it from its slumber. A dazzling bright light blinded me.

I squinted and looked away, allowing my pupils to adjust to the sudden brilliance in the blackness. When I could finally sort of look at my phone through lidded eyes, I did not even bother to find the flashlight app. The light from the screen was enough for my purposes.

I clambered to my feet and held the phone out before me as if it was a charm to ward off evil spirits. A narrow throw of illumination revealed an oblique section of the living room surrounded by inky gloom. I pointed the phone at various spots around the room, lighting up my furniture. At any moment, I expected a strange face to appear, possibly grinning a death mask at me, raising a knife or a crowbar or a baseball bat to bring about my quick demise—

"Is anybody there?" I tried to shout, but my voice croaked a crackling whisper. "Come out where I can see you."

Movement caught my eye. I retreated. My back hit the counter separating this room from the kitchen.

"Wh-who's there?"

A sigh. I heard it distinctly. There was someone else in the house with me. I could feel his presence. It filled the atmosphere as clearly as the stink of cooking cabbage fills a nasal passage.

A footstep. He was approaching me from the shadowy recesses of my home. This invader, this trespasser, this violator was here with me. I still could not see him, but I knew he was just outside the faint beam from my phone.

A rustle. He must have been readying his weapon, preparing for the attack. I froze in place, a statue with a pounding heart and inoperable limbs. When the assault began, I was sure I'd succumb.

Then I saw him—his face drifted into the light. Glowing eyes surrounded by a dark mask stared at me. Sharp teeth bared in a gruesome grin. Tiny, clawed fingers reached out.

I screamed.

The raccoon darted across the floor and scampered through the kitchen. The trash can crashed down, and I heard its contents scatter everywhere. Then a *THWICK THWACK* echoed through the now empty residence.

A relief laugh escaped my lips and my body slumped over the counter. I had forgotten about the doggy door we had installed for my Golden Retriever. I never saw the need to replace it—I was too lazy, or perhaps I hoped that the dog and its owner would someday return.

It was time to close that door for good.

REFLECTIONS BY A POND

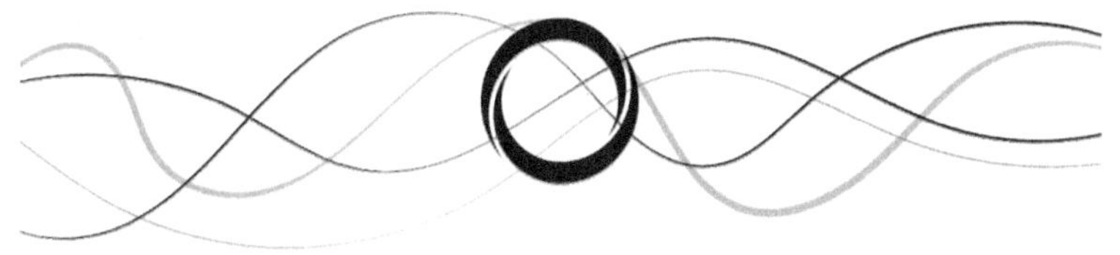

Dead.

Jordan Bennett could not wrap his head around the concept. It was incomprehensible that his best friend was no longer alive. It could not be possible.

He sat with his back against the rough bark of an oak near the edge of a glistening pond. Overhead, two parallel branches reached out like arms awaiting an embrace. The higher bough was the perfect height to grasp while inching across the lower limb on a hot day, intending to leap into the cool water below. Years before, someone had nailed several planks into the trunk to make a ladder for easy climbing. Those boards were now half rotten and the nails were rusty. Maybe some enterprising youth will replace them some day and make summer plunges safe for another generation.

While Jordan's hands absently clawed at the dirt and tufts of grass growing in the tree's shade, his fingers located a round stone. He threw it side-arm at the pond, where it skipped on the glassy surface and left little rings of ripples as it bounced three, four times before disappearing into the water. After a moment, the wavelets were gone, as if they had never even existed. Like Ryan.

The two boys met when they were in seventh grade. Five years later, they were inseparable. Graduation was coming up in a month. The thought of walking through the ceremony without Ryan there was too much for Jordan, and another bout of grief erupted in him. He buried his red and swollen eyes in the crook of his arm, letting his tears soak into the sleeve of his dress shirt.

The funeral was a blur, like a bad dream that dissipates upon regaining consciousness—the residual feeling of depression and desperation was still there, but the specifics were a confused jumble in Jordan's mind. He didn't want to go, but his mother made him. She said that it was his duty as Ryan's friend. What would Ryan's parents think if he skipped out? Jordan thought it would be too overwhelming for him to endure. However, the service ended up being a gauzy play with the participants pretending that a tragedy had occurred. The problem was that the curtains did not close, the actors did not bow, the audience did not applaud. Life continued—at least for him.

The casket was open for viewing. Jordan was frightened to approach, but his mother escorted him. The waxy thing lying on the silk padding sort of resembled Ryan, but was lacking any sense that this was an actual human being. Absent was any sign of the teen's vibrant personality or biting sense of humor. His face lay slack, expressionless.

This was just a mannequin, a store-front exhibit selling coffins.

The one thing it proved, though, was how wrong and downright ludicrous some rumors were. The kids in school loved to talk, even if they had no idea what was fact or fiction. Unfortunately, fantasy seemed to be much more interesting and was often treated as reality. Some believed that Ryan had been decapitated. Others alleged he was impaled with a tree, a stop sign, or even the steering column. Yet another report was the certainty that he burned alive. The truth was much more mundane—the coroner concluded that the cause of death was a broken neck. Even though the airbag had deployed upon impact, Ryan had not worn his seat belt. Jordan learned of this by eavesdropping on whispered conversations by his parents.

After the funeral, Jordan wandered down through his subdivision without bothering to change out of his black suit. He didn't remember reaching the trailhead and making his way to the pond, but found himself staring into the reflection of the trees lining the waterline, with his suit jacket draped over one shoulder. He acknowledged his new location with as much regard as a fly does when finding itself in a kitchen. This was one of his and Ryan's favorite hangout spots, so it was natural that his feet had taken him here.

One phrase echoed through his mind. It latched onto his thoughts like a white blood cell devouring a virus.

Drunk driver.

Teenagers believe they are impervious to many things. Drinking and driving is one of a long list of horrors that happen to *other* people, including such unpleasantries as unwanted pregnancies, AIDS, cancer, and mental illness. Jordan listened to warnings of the dangers of DUIs, but it never occurred to him that this would affect his life in any meaningful way. It was unfathomable that alcohol would end the life of someone so close to him.

"Why?" he called out to the woods.

That was the question, wasn't it? It is what everyone who suffers devastation and misfortune asks. Why did this happen? What is the purpose? If there is to be meaning to life, how do you subscribe significance to such a pointless event?

Jordan pictured Ryan standing in front of him, his lanky frame slouched in that devil-may-care attitude of his; a smirk on his face that said he had a private joke he was hiding from the world; hair hanging in his eyes, making him look like the sheepdog from the Looney Toons cartoons.

"Why'd you have to die?"

The spectral figure of Ryan flipped his hair out of his eyes that twinkled with a sign that he was about to zing a poor victim with an acerbic witticism.

"Oh, poor Jordan, boo hoo," Ryan said in Jordan's head. "I'm dead and you're alive, and you feel sorry for yourself. How do you think *I* feel?"

Yes, Jordan could imagine Ryan saying this very thing.

"How else do you expect me to feel? Want me to dance in the streets?"

"I've seen your moves. Trust me, no one wants you to dance in the streets. You're like a squirrel with hiccups."

Jordan barked a harsh snort of mirth, an alien sound in his ears. He thought about the first dance he attended. It was the end of eighth grade and he had a huge crush on a girl named Jenny Sanderson, but was deathly afraid to talk to her. Ryan wrung this information out of him and swore he'd take the secret to the grave. That promise lasted all of about twelve hours. In the middle of Language Arts, while the class was reading *The Giver*, Ryan volunteered to recite a passage. He was an excellent reader, able to provide inflection to words far beyond the halting monotone that characterized most kids struggling to verbalize the words on the page. When he volunteered for a turn, the students released a collective sigh of relief—one that was shared by the teacher, a large, jovial woman named Mrs. Long.

"'Almost every citizen in the community had dark eyes. His parents did, and Lily did, and so did all of his group members and friends. But there were a few exceptions.' Jordan is madly in love with Jenny Sanderson and wants to take her to the dance. The world would crash down around him if she turned him down, and he'd have to spend the entire night playing *Call of Duty* while crying on his controller."

At first, the class was confused, thinking they had lost the passage, or that Ryan had skipped a paragraph. Then when they realized he was no longer reading but was speaking about real people—other kids in the very classroom—snickers and giggles spread through the room. Poor Jenny Sanderson turned bright red and covered her face with her hands. Jordan turned more of a shade of purple and wanted to tear into Ryan on the spot. He would *never* forgive him for embarrassing him this way. For the rest of the period, Jordan fumed. Nothing else about Lois Lowry's book penetrated his skull, which throbbed with anger and shame.

Ryan looked pleased with himself. "I'm sorry, Mrs. Long,

I lost my place." This caused a peal of laughter from his classmates that Mrs. Long had to squash. Like most of the teachers, she liked Ryan and often put up with his antics.

After class, Jordan gathered up his belongings quickly to make a hasty exit before anyone could confront him about whether his world would really end if Jenny did not go with him to the dance. He spun around while still cramming books into his backpack and nearly collided with the subject of his unrequited affections.

"Do you really want to go to the dance with me?" Jenny asked. Her smile could have been from flattery or mockery. Jordan couldn't tell which.

"Um...Ryan's a jerk."

"I'm not going with anyone. Yet." And that was that. Jordan had his first date, thanks to the irrepressible Ryan Alvarez.

"You don't have to thank me," Ryan said in the hallway as Jordan hurried to his next period.

"I should punch you," Jordan replied. The threat carried little weight, since he was grinning like a lottery winner.

The dance itself was nerve-wracking. Jordan didn't know how to dress, what to say, and—most importantly—how to dance. He stumbled during the slow dances and felt like an epilepsy patient during the fast ones. However, the one thing he learned was that Jenny Sanderson was dull. Once he got over the initial shock of actually being with a girl who voluntarily wanted to spend an evening with him, he discovered she had the intelligence of a bullfrog and the depth of a spring puddle. That she was beautiful kept her interesting for about an hour and a half, and by the end of the night, Jenny had drifted away to be with her friends, and

Jordan latched onto Ryan until their parents picked them up.

"I could always count on you to get me in trouble," Jordan said, skipping another stone across the pond. "I never had the guts to do anything."

"That's for sure, you wimp. What are you gonna do without me?"

Jordan wondered if this was a sign of insanity. He could actually hear Ryan, as if he were really standing next to him. His voice was as real as the birds twittering in the branches overhead. He thought that if he reached out, he could actually touch his friend. Maybe this was Ryan's ghost, having returned one last time to say goodbye—or to haunt him. If so, he could think of worse things to experience.

"You were supposed to be a high-priced attorney." To say that Ryan had a sharp mind was an understatement—his I.Q. tests were off the charts. He was in the Gifted program in school and A.P. classes in high school. Jordan shared most of those classes with him, but had to work hard to keep up while Ryan breezed through. In fact, he qualified for college credits and was well on his way toward his Associate's Degree at seventeen. Ryan was the best member of the debate team (he referred to himself as a master debater) and had every intention of going to law school, though he was undecided if he'd be a criminal lawyer or one of those crusaders trying to stop evil corporations from screwing over the population. He even told Ryan that maybe one day he'd run for president. Jordan was certain that he would.

"Yeah, well, you were supposed to be a dork. Oh, look! You succeeded!"

"Is that how you're going to haunt me? By insulting me?"

"What better way to spend eternity?"

"You're an ass."

"Yes, but I'm your ass." Ryan said this in such a solemn manner that Jordan couldn't help but burst out laughing. The corner of Ryan's mouth turned up slightly. He rarely laughed out loud, but held his amusement on the inside while causing others to express their own merriment. Jordan knew him well enough to know that the position of Ryan's mouth revealed the level of his enjoyment—biting his lip, allowing both corners to upturn, or actually showing teeth.

When Jordan regained control of himself, he said, "Remember Mrs. Sauer's Science class?"

Ryan's eyes cocked to the side, and he allowed his two front teeth to rest on his lower lip. "Oh yeah. The movies." The Science teacher spent half of her time showing videos to the class. Spurred on by Ryan, Jordan took part in ridiculing every presentation. They reached a point where they had running commentary throughout the films that were much more entertaining to the surrounding students than what was on the TV screen.

"Mrs. Sauer never said a *thing* to us." Jordan planted his face in one palm. "At the end of the year, she wrote a note on my report card that she had never heard anyone talk in class as much as me. Me!"

Ryan allowed himself a slight, silent chuckle. "Normally you'd have to be threatened within an inch of your life to make a sound in class."

"Yeah, that's your influence on me. A bad influence."

"I was a horrible role model. You're better off without me."

"You got me in so much trouble."

"So you said."

"*You* could get away with murder. Everybody loved you."

"Not Mr. Hawkins." Ryan rolled his eyes as he said the name. Mr. Hawkins was the athletic director at the high school and taught P.E. to both Jordan and Ryan. While Jordan was the furthest thing from an athlete, Ryan was pretty decent at most sports—not a jock, but showed promise if he put his mind to it. The problem was that he hadn't been interested in playing on any team, and Mr. Hawkins resented it. Acting like he took Ryan's rejection personally, he took out his frustration on the boy.

"I think he had a crush on you."

"He'd break your kneecap if he heard you say that."

"He can go suck a toad." Ryan constantly came up with new and innovative ways of cussing, not being satisfied with the normal, boring vulgarities. Jordan repeated these oaths, and this one was his favorite. Another popular swear was "jackalope nipples."

Jordan regressed into his own thoughts and sat for a while, not speaking. He stared at the sparse clouds glide by overhead. It was a warm and humid day, but showed no signs of rain in the immediate future. He felt sticky and sweaty. The pond looked inviting. Of course, without a bathing suit, he would have to strip down to his boxers for a dip, and he would not do that. He never felt comfortable showing off his body in public. He knew that Ryan would have no problem at all going *au naturel* if the need arose— and had on at least one occasion.

The two had attended a party, much like on the night of the accident, where parents were gone, kids got a hold of booze, and wildness ensued. It was, in fact, the first time that Ryan became publicly inebriated. He had downed several beers, which was enough for his inexperienced body to become saturated with the spirits. Someone dared him to jump into the pool, and he gladly accepted the challenge despite the night air being chilly. As he pulled his socks and shoes from his feet, the partygoers chanted, "Take it off! Take it off!" He complied and performed an unbalanced dive to a round of cheers before clambering out of the icy water and streaking into the house for warmth. Jordan drove him home that night, laughing the entire way at his friend's drunken antics.

Jordan did not care for alcohol himself, though had experimented with it at Ryan's insistence. At age fifteen, the two found themselves alone at Ryan's house one night while his parents were out until the wee hours of the morning. Ryan raided the liquor cabinet and urged Jordan to join him in taste-testing each of the various multicolored bottles. At every swallow, Jordan felt like spitting out the toxic liquid while Ryan took to it like a slug to mucus. Jordan joined his buddy in several other secretive drinking sessions, but during those times, he usually just nursed a beer while watching and laughing at Ryan's increasing intoxication. Ryan was fun and funny normally, but with the help of alcohol, he was hilarity incarnate. These incidents happened infrequently, so there was never a concern about addiction. Ryan was too smart for that.

Snapping out of his reverie, Jordan expected Ryan to have vanished—after all, he was just a figment of Jordan's injured imagination. His muddled mind had produced a representation of his friend, nothing more.

Ryan gazed down at him, a patient and pleasant expression on his face.

"Still here?" Jordan knew that if anyone wandered by, that person would think that he had lost touch with reality by talking to the air. The simple fact was that Ryan did not exist.

"Disappointed?" the imaginary Ryan asked.

"Naw. Just thought I wouldn't have to look at your ugly face again."

"I'll be gone soon enough. You'll forget what my ugly face looks like. And with your mental skills, you'll be lucky to remember my name. You'll be like, 'What's his name? Rick? Randy?'" He snapped his fingers twice. "'Ryan! No, wait, is that right?'"

Jordan blew air through his lips. "Not likely. You've burned a permanent brand on my brain."

Tired of sitting, Jordan pushed himself to his feet and brushed off the seat of his pants. He stood several inches shorter than Ryan, who had "shot up like a weed," as Jordan's mom put it, when he was 14. Jordan never quite caught up, growing incrementally each year. He was still waiting for that proverbial growth spurt, which the doctor said could happen anytime, even into his twenties. His dad was of average height, so he did not expect to remain short all his life. It was just annoying waiting for nature to take its course.

Deep down inside, he recognized that hint of jealousy toward his best friend. In many ways, Ryan was the person he wanted to be and never would be. One reason he enjoyed watching Ryan get drunk was the loss of control, the proof that Ryan was not perfect. This was one instance where Jordan was superior to him, remaining sober while Ryan degenerated into drunkenness. Most of the time, though, Jordan was content with just sharing Ryan's life—being Ryan by proxy—and now that was gone.

"What happened that night?"

Ryan blinked twice, showing that he didn't know how to answer. He never admitted ignorance or confusion, but just remained silent.

"Did you fall asleep at the wheel? Or were you just too wasted to notice the curve?" No one knew the answer to this, despite speculations. The road made a sharp right turn, but Ryan's car had gone straight while traveling at 110 miles per hour. Trees caught the vehicle and transformed it into a twisted bundle of metal and glass. Ryan's blood alcohol level had been twice the legal limit, but it was undetermined whether he was conscious during the wreck.

"Why do you wanna talk about that?" Did Jordan detect a hint of defensiveness in his voice?

"You shouldn't have driven that night."

"Shoulda woulda coulda."

"You weren't supposed to die, damn it!" Jordan recoiled at the vehemence in his own voice.

"I had to get home before my parents did. If they saw me come home trashed, they would've been pissed."

"That worked out great."

"Why didn't you drive me? You always drive me when I'm drunk."

"Because..." Jordan's voice hitched. "I wanted to stay."

Ryan had been popular among most of the kids in

school, including those in higher grades. As a senior, he kept in touch with those who had graduated the previous year or two through various social media sites, and a guy who was now in college invited him to a party with other college students. Of course, Ryan brought along Jordan.

To Jordan's surprise, he actually enjoyed himself despite being out of his normal peer group. This was a new crowd, more mature than his usual circle of high school acquaintances. It was exciting for him, and he wanted to make the most of it.

Of course, the best way to win over new people was through his association with Ryan. What better way for Ryan to liven up a party than to be under the influence...

"I got you drunk," Jordan mumbled. His vision blurred. He could not read Ryan's expression. "I wanted you to be fun, so I gave you a beer. And kept giving them to you. Until you were plastered."

He turned toward the tree and placed his forehead against it. He didn't care that the bark was surely leaving indentions in his skin.

"It's my fault that you died."

Jordan felt a hand on his shoulder. The touch was gentle, but the pressure firm. Whatever part of his mind formed this hallucination did a good job mimicking human contact.

Ryan's voice was soothing, his breath tickling the hairs at the base of Jordan's neck. While he typically acted like an aloof intellectual jester, he could be surprisingly sensitive and supportive when needed—even if that was a rarity. "Dude, you're not responsible."

The tears flowed freely, and Jordan didn't even try to stop them. "I killed you."

Jordan found himself whirled around. Ryan's face was inches from his own and was livid.

"You friggin' idiot! You think you could make me do anything? Can you think of one time that you actually forced me to do something I didn't want to do?"

He had a point. Jordan could not think of one example. On the contrary, Jordan was constantly following Ryan's lead. "No," he admitted.

"Then stop being a dumbass by blaming yourself. *I* willingly drank those beers, *I* knowingly got drunk, and *I* stupidly attempted to drive home in that condition. If I wanted you to drive me home, don't you think I would've manipulated you into doing it?"

"Yeah, probably."

"Probably? Wake up, Jordan. You know better than that."

"You're right."

"Of course I'm right. I always am."

"You're so arrogant."

"Was." Ryan's famous smirk returned.

"Whatever."

An uncharacteristically serious expression crossed Ryan's face. "I really screwed up this time, didn't I?"

"Yeah."

"Sorry it turned out this way." He turned and peered out at the pond. Jordan joined him at his side. "We had some good times here, didn't we?"

"Uh huh. I remember that time you did the belly smacker jumping off the tree. You were in so much pain. Your whole chest and stomach was solid red."

"Good times."

Black bugs danced on the surface tension of the water

like swarming polka dots. At some point, the pond took on a rusty tint, and Jordan realized it was a reflection of the setting sun. He did not know how long he stood there gaping at his childhood swimming hole, the place that held most of the fond memories of his friendship with Ryan. He turned to his friend to say something.

Ryan was gone, if indeed he was ever there.

Jordan exhaled a long breath, gathered up his jacket from the ground, and headed home.

HAPPY CAMPER

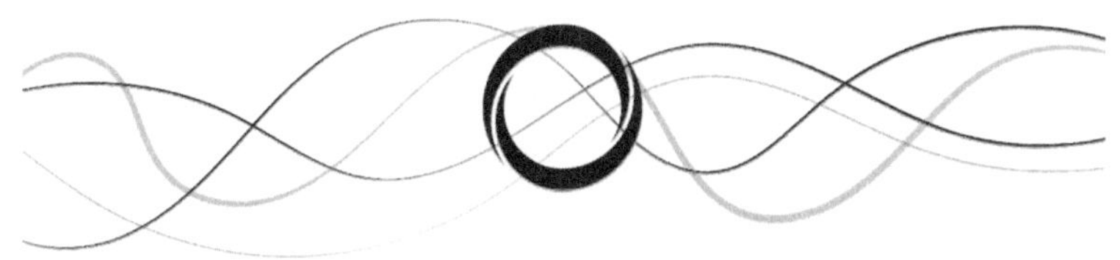

ow did I end up here? Ronnie mentally muttered as he looked around the clearing in the woods. He had avoided the dreaded ritual of camping for all of his twenty-four years, but somehow his buddies talked him into it against his wishes. So much for peer pressure ending in high school.

The sun had gone down behind the tree line, throwing long shadows in every which direction because of the tangle of branches knit together like a knobby lattice overhead. Familiar sounds of the city were absent, replaced with the hollow whoosh of wind passing through the boughs high above and the high-pitched bird calls that seemed to come from hidden speakers all around. The overbearing pollen that filled the air plugged up Ronnie's sinus cavity and brought watery redness to his eyes. He was happy he couldn't smell the stench of animal droppings and decomposing plant matter that must waft in unseen clouds from the forest.

"Wanna gimme a hand?" Jerry asked from the bed of the pickup truck.

Ronnie plodded back to the vehicle with pins and needles stabbing through his legs as circulation returned. He had been squashed in what passed for a back seat in the truck for the last hour. His legs were not long, but the lack of room back there caused him to eat his knees.

Before Ronnie could even get all the way to the battered truck that fit right in with this environment, his stocky companion hurled a bag-enclosed tent at him. Reaction time was never one of Ronnie's strengths, and the tent bounced off his chest and landed on the ground. The poles inside the bag rattled together angrily.

"Fumble!" Jerry's whole fleshy torso bobbling as he chortled. He was a master wit.

As Ronnie stood back up after picking the tent off the ground, his peripheral vision registered yet another incoming missile spiraling toward him. He winced and attempted to do a turtle maneuver by pulling his head as far into his chest as anatomy allowed. Fortunately, it was enough for the rolled-up sleeping bag to zip past his face without making contact.

"Heads up," Jerry warned after the fact.

"Thanks," Ronnie mumbled. He grumbled, "Why'd we have to come out here, anyway?"

"Fresh air's good for you." Jerry tossed him a duffel bag, which Ronnie caught with a sudden expulsion of air. "Maybe put some life in that pasty body of yours."

Once the truck was unloaded, the third member of their

group, Samuel, strode into the clearing, apparently from nowhere. Tall and limber, he exuded an air of quiet confidence that Ronnie secretly found repulsive. Though he would never express this verbally, he often wished that Samuel would make some mistake in his life. Just one.

"The trail leads down to a pond," Samuel's smooth voice intoned. "There's a dock that looks good for fishing. We could probably do some swimming later if you guys want."

"Who knows what kind of bacteria is in that thing?" Ronnie whined. "And I didn't bring my nose plug."

"I can plug it for ya." Jerry pounded his fist into an open palm for punctuation, but chuckled to show that it was all a joke. Ronnie suspected Jerry would probably chuckle the same way as he pounded that fist into Ronnie's nose.

They carried the gear into the clearing and separated it into piles, one for each of the guys and a fourth for community equipment like the pop-up fly to go over the kitchen area and the accompanying gear—a folding table, a camping stove, bottles of propane, a water jug, a cooler, and a plastic tote full of utensils and other gadgets they might need during the weekend.

Jerry and Samuel set about assembling their tents. Ronnie, meanwhile, dumped all the pieces out of the bag and onto the ground. He stared at the bundle of nylon amid an octopus of sectional plastic poles held together by an internal bungee. He stared at the heap, with no clue what to do with it all.

"You okay over there?" the musical chords of Samuel's voice sang. Ronnie forced himself not to recoil at its horrendous melody.

"I'm fine." To illustrate his fineness, Ronnie picked up a

tent pole, which flopped about like a lance that has seen one too many jousts. He attached two of the segments together, surprising himself at the accomplishment. Soon, he snapped together the entire length of the pole and beheld it proudly.

The other two tents stood like bloated toads, mocking his single achievement. Ronnie's narrow shoulders slouched with disappointment as he pondered how those guys could have possibly set up their tents so quickly. That thought bounced around his brain for the next twenty minutes as he tried vainly to figure out how the poles connected to the tent. He tried to tune out the sound of Jerry's hyucks as he sat in his folding chair, being entertained by Ronnie's non-existent tent-building skills. Finally, Samuel joined him without a word and patiently guided the poles through the proper sleeves in the tent and like magic, the tent rose into the air majestically. The last step was to cover it with the fly, which snapped across the top of the tent with ease. Ronnie fumed at how stupid he was that he couldn't figure it out.

"Just takes practice, that's all," Samuel trumpeted. He stretched his six-foot-four frame with his muscled arms reaching for the clouds and let out a satisfied growl of content. Sunlight peeked through the trees at just the right angle for a golden ray to strike his tousled sandy hair and set it aglow. His shadow fell on Ronnie, whose lower back grabbed him as he staggered to his feet while emitting a squeak of discomfort.

Ronnie stowed his belongings inside the tent, then fought with his sleeping bag to remove it from its plastic carrying case. He had just purchased it from Walmart, having never needed a sleeping bag until now. Samuel offered to let him use one of his spares, just like he loaned Ronnie the tent, but Ronnie just couldn't bring himself to sleep inside something that another guy had slept in. There was no telling how much sweat, dead skin cells, hair, and who-knows-what-else had been deposited in the cloth padding. The thought of how unsanitary it was made him want to retch.

Having gotten the arrangement inside the tent to his relative satisfaction, Ronnie joined the other two outside and set up his folding chair. Surprisingly, it was a fairly simple task. Samuel and Jerry were engaged in a heated discussion of a football team, a topic that Ronnie had no interest in participating. Instead, he took out his smart phone and touched the icon for the Internet.

"That ain't gonna work." Jerry's smirk was evident in his tone of voice, and when Ronnie looked up at him, the smirk was confirmed. "No signal out here."

"I know there's no wi-fi," Ronnie said with indignation. "I'm using my data plan."

Jerry spewed a "hyuck hyuck" before saying, "That don't matter. Cell phones don't work out here. At all."

"You mean I can't even make a phone call?"

"That's what it means, Einstein."

"But I've gotta check Facebook."

"Not tonight, you're not. Hyuck hyuck."

"You never said I wouldn't be able to use my phone."

Jerry shrugged, sending a ripple through the jelly-like rolls on his neck. "Now you know."

"Sorry, Ronnie," Samuel piped. "I should've told you. I'm so used to it I forget to prepare others who don't have experience." A breeze passed through the campsite and brushed his locks away from his face like a curtain, exposing a strong slab of a forehead above his piercing blue eyes.

"It's okay," Ronnie conceded, taking off his glasses to wipe the sweat off of the bridge of his pimply nose. He stood. "Where's the bathroom?"

Samuel hooked a thumb toward a small trail in the opposite direction from the truck. "The outhouse is over there."

"Outhouse?" Ronnie dreaded the sound of that, even if Samuel's reedy voice made the word sound pleasant.

"You don't know what an outhouse is?" Jerry blew air and spittle through his teeth derisively.

"I *know* what an outhouse is. You mean to say that there's no flush toilet?"

"Just a hole in the ground." Jerry demonstrated by spreading out his hands in a roughly circular shape and peered through it. "Plop, plop, fizz, fizz, oh what a relief it is! Hyuck hyuck hyuck."

"Do you even know what that's from?" Ronnie asked. The best defense was an offense.

Jerry stopped in mid-hyuck. "Um..."

Ronnie put his hands on his hips like a grandmother scolding a young child. "It's from an old commercial. You always say things without knowing what they even mean. How'd you even make it through college?"

Jerry rocked his bulk forward in what was supposed to be a menacing manner, but the chair moved with him, clamped to his ample bottom. "Excuse me, Mister Pop Culture Reference, for not knowing every obscure fact from television history. Oh, look! I used a big word. However, did I know how to do that?"

Samuel interceded before escalation became more severe. "Guys, come on. We're supposed to be out here to enjoy ourselves. Kick back, relax, be one with nature. All that crap."

Music soothed the beasts, and both Ronnie and Jerry calmed down.

Jerry threw out a peace offering. "If the outhouse bothers you that much, I got a shovel. Just go out behind a bush somewhere and be one with nature."

The thought of doing his business in a hole in the middle of the wilderness out in the open for anyone to see was less appealing to Ronnie than dealing with a non-flushable latrine, but he held his tongue for the sake of peace.

"Just be careful you don't squat over poison ivy," Jerry added.

"Poison ivy?" Ronnie scratched his arm as if the mere thought of the plant was enough to infect him. "I'll use the outhouse."

The building in question was constructed by a two-by-four frame surrounded by aging plywood walls with strips peeled off from it, leaving the top portion looking like jagged, rotting teeth. These walls left a three-inch gap between both the ceiling and the ground. A sheet of corrugated aluminum topped the structure at an angle to allow rain to drain away from the door, which did not close all the way.

Inside, Ronnie found the cramped room to be full of spider-webs. In fact, the architect of one batch still lived in the corner—a black, hairy arachnid the size of a quarter but with spindly legs that stretched out double the length of its body. It eyed Ronnie as he stepped onto the sagging floor, and Ronnie guarded himself from any impromptu attacks. His urge to evacuate was stronger than the fear of being bitten.

A stained and cracked toilet seat surrounded a hole that looked large enough to swallow a man if he wasn't careful. Ronnie peered down into it and was happy to see that darkness hid the contents below. The smell was as rank as he expected, its vapors penetrating his clogged sinuses like a bullet through a balloon.

Upon finishing his bodily requirements, he spared no time in rushing out into the fresh air, which buffeted his senses like a gaseous battering ram. Momentary panic overtook him, however, as he lost track of the trail leading back to camp. Then he remembered he had approached the outhouse square on with the door, so all he had to do was stand in front of it and look forward. The line of hard-packed soil amid ankle-high grass appeared like an image in a magic eye poster.

Samuel and Jerry halted their discussion of which wings place had hotter waitresses as Ronnie crashed into the clearing.

"Guess everything came out okay," Jerry snickered, minus his hyucks this time.

RONNIE WAS DISTRESSED BY HOW FAST THE TEMPERATURE DROPPED once night fell. He sat as close to the campfire as he dared, hugging himself to keep warm and trying to ignore Jerry's taunting reminder to bring a jacket. Of course, Ronnie didn't see the need as he had no clue that away from civilization, the air was ten degrees colder than in the city.

The fire crackled. A flickering orange hue blanketed the campsite, giving the others a sickly citrus skin tone. Ronnie rubbed his hands together, trying to rid them of the layer of grime that had caked on when he helped gather firewood. The pads on his hands were tender, and he was sure ugly calluses would form. He didn't like calluses, and he liked less the activities that caused them.

Smoke invaded his nostrils, making him cough. He moved his chair over. This was his third time moving the chair to avoid the noxious fumes from the flame, which seemed to follow him. Before long, he will have made a full rotation around the pit.

Samuel's long fingers strummed his guitar. He hummed a heavenly melody, surely just to show off his musical proficiency. After all, he must constantly prove to the world how he was the best at everything, how much better of a *man* he was—at least compared to Ronnie, who tried to prevent himself from being carried away by the clarity and splendor of the tune. He failed.

An intense, needle-like jab stabbed him in the neck. "Ow!" He slapped at the pain, then saw a blood smear across his palm. The carcass of a mosquito lay amid the gruesome splash. The edges of his mouth cranked down into a repulsed frown as he searched frantically for something to wipe the horror from his hand. Before he could locate anything worthy of the task, another mosquito dive-bombed his temple. His soiled hand reacted involuntarily, resulting in a blood smear like a war wound across Ronnie's forehead.

He jumped to his feet and swiped at the air in a frenzy. "I hate mosquitoes!"

"Who doesn't?" Jerry rolled his eyes as if that were the most obvious observation ever made by humanity. He tossed him a can of bug spray, which bounced off of Ronnie's hands. "Here."

"Don't let that get too close to the fire," Samuel sang, not interrupting his guitar mastery. "I told you not to bring aerosol. They explode."

Jerry's eyes lit up. "Yeah."

"Oh, great." *SLAP!* Another mosquito bit the dust, this time as its syringe-like proboscis was embedded in what passed as Ronnie's upper arm muscle. The insect's fat, blood-filled body exploded upon impact, leaving Ronnie now with two crimson palms. He held them out in front of him, on the verge of tears. *How am I going to clean them?*

On the table, he found the large dispenser of hand sanitizer he insisted on bringing, despite the other guys telling him it was unnecessary. He squirted a huge glob of the viscous liquid into his palms and massaged his hands together, generating a gooey lather. The strong disinfectant stung his eyes, and he rubbed them until he realized he would only make it worse. Instead, he blinked rapidly. Hand sanitizer, Ronnie discovered, did not wash away grunge, but only left his hands with a layer of ooze on his skin that mixed with the dirt, blood, and mosquito remains that covered his appendages. He gave up and wiped his hands on his pants.

"I'm going to bed." With that, he marched to his tent, battled the zipper on the door flap, and climbed in. He slid into his sleeping bag feet first, wiggling his narrow hips to shimmy into the warm cocoon like a snake shedding its skin in reverse.

Sleep did not come easily. A root or a rock—Ronnie could not tell which—was directly under his sleeping bag and no amount of pushing at it through the bottom of the tent would budge it. Ronnie had to move his sleeping bag in the dark.

He lay on the hard ground for an eternity, trying to get comfortable. Every position he tried resulted in moments of achy stillness before he shifted to another awkward angle. On his back, on his side, on his other side, on his stomach—it didn't matter. His body was just not meant to sleep on anything except a soft mattress.

Conversation and music from his companions ended as they took to their respective tents. The night air became quiet—too quiet. Ronnie became acutely aware that he was in the middle of nowhere, with no means of communication. He hated horror movies, especially the slasher variety, but regardless, the idea of a masked serial killer stalking the woods invaded his consciousness, no matter how ridiculous the concept was. That concern turned to one of a more practical matter—wildlife. What if a bear or a rabid raccoon decided it wanted to climb inside with him? This tent was no protection against the razor-sharp claws and teeth. Random scenarios of vicious animals attacking him in his sleep, or lack thereof, played out on the television in his mind. But it was a much smaller threat that became the true nuisance.

A mosquito had somehow entered the tent. It had enacted its cloaking device because Ronnie could not locate the pest visually—the only evidence of its existence was the buzzing that started off as a low hum off in the recesses of the shelter, but then grew in volume and intensity as the aerial assailant swooped in for its surveillance of its intended feast. The jet engine sound rattled in Ronnie's eardrum, causing him to smack his ear repeatedly in a vain attempt to stifle that nerve-wracking racket. The only recourse was for Ronnie to bury his head inside his sleeping bag, though after about ten minutes of breathing his own heated exhalations, the atmosphere within his shroud became unbearable and he had to expose his head once again to the invisible bombardier.

Eventually, the annoyance of the imperceptible mosquito was overtaken by a thunderous chorus of creatures—crickets, tree frogs, chupacabras—Ronnie didn't know and didn't care. All he knew was that thousands of tiny fingers were scratching blackboards all around his tent, and the creators of this ungodly din were enjoying it to no end.

At some point, Ronnie must have fallen asleep, because a loud *HHHOOOOO* right above him startled him awake. His body lurched at the sudden screech and landed with a thud on the hard ground. He took several deep breaths and pulled the edge of the sleeping bag up over his mouth and nose, leaving his wide eyes exposed to discern any intruder in the dark. He heard a rustle, a flap of enormous wings, and then the night was still again. It took a long while of staring at the shadows that danced on the nylon ceiling above him, cast by moonlight through the trees before sleep claimed Ronnie once more.

Morning arrived far too soon. Ronnie attempted to climb out of the tent, but became entangled in the partially unzipped flap door. He finally freed himself of the complexity of a swath of nylon and a zipper and stood in an empty campsite. Tendrils of smoke wafted up from the charred remains of last night's campfire. The air was chilly —enough to raise goose bumps on Ronnie's arms—yet was refreshing and pure, unlike the air conditioning that artificially cooled his apartment and left it stale and impersonal. Somehow, Ronnie's senses were vivid. He realized that the sun had not yet crested the trees, and upon looking at the clock on his cell phone, he saw it was a mere 6:23. Normally, he would not be awake this early unless he had a very important appointment.

Voices cut through the light mist that hovered among the trees. Ronnie followed them down a trail, only stumbling twice in his not-quite-awake state. His muscles were sore and knotted, and did not respond well to what his foggy mind demanded of them.

He discovered Samuel and Jerry fishing from a long, rickety dock that protruded over a good-sized body of water. It was not quite a lake, but was big enough for Ronnie to be wary of it. Fear of drowning kept him away from anything deeper than his knees.

"Hiya," Jerry said as he cast his line a dozen feet into the water.

"We thought we'd let you sleep in." Samuel sounded stuffed up, like a muted jazz trumpet.

"This is sleeping in?" Ronnie murmured.

Jerry held out his fishing rod. "Wanna give it a try?"

"No, thanks." Ronnie's dad took him fishing exactly one time when he was eleven. It bored him to tears. Why anyone wanted to stand for hours throwing a pole around, hoping a fish would bite into a hook and tear a hole in its cheek, was beyond him. What would you do after you caught the fish? Cut it open and rip out its guts? Definitely not for Ronnie. If you threw the fish back in the water, then what was the point of catching it in the first place?

He sat on the grass and watched the non-action of his friends fishing until ants climbing on his flesh took a nibble. He returned to the camp.

Not long after, Samuel and Jerry trotted up the trail sans fish. "Fish ain't biting," Jerry sighed. "Guess no dinner tonight."

This distressed Ronnie. "What do you mean, no dinner? You mean you were going to *catch* dinner? We were going to eat something from that pond?"

"Calm down," Samuel crooned. "He was just kidding. We got the meals covered. In fact, we're going to make breakfast now that you're up."

Ronnie glared at Jerry, whose shoulders quaked with silent laughter at Ronnie's expense.

Breakfast turned out to be omelets with hash browns and sausage patties. Samuel had pre-prepped various veggies with diced tomatoes, onions, green peppers, and mushrooms, plus shredded cheese in their own zip-lock baggies so each guy could choose his own fixings to make his omelet to meet his taste. They took turns whisking the eggs in a plastic bowl and then pouring it into a pan placed on a burner on the propane stove. The other burner had a pan to cook bacon and potatoes. Samuel produced a jug of fresh orange juice from the cooler. While the ambiance had a lot to be desired, Ronnie found the meal to be quite tasty, especially after a dollop of hot sauce on the eggs.

Cleanup proved less of a challenge than Ronnie had feared. Being germ-minded, he worried about leaving dirty dishes lying about all day to allow bacteria to fester. However, Samuel heated a pot of water and poured it into two plastic tubs, then added liquid detergent to the first tub. A third one contained cold water, into which Samuel dispensed a capful of bleach. He explained that the soapy water was, of course, for washing, followed by hot water to rinse. The cold bleach water was to sanitize the dishes. This intrigued Ronnie and relieved him of his distress over health concerns. He washed his plastic plate and utensils, then placed them on a towel spread on the table to dry.

After breakfast, the plan was to go on a hike, which displeased Ronnie to no end. "What's the point of walking to nowhere and then just coming back?

"Exercise. It's good for you." Jerry did not appear to take his own suggestion often.

"You can experience nature." Samuel spread his arms wide, as if conducting an orchestra composed of the flora surrounding the camp. "You'd be amazed at what you can see while hiking."

Yeah, trees, thought Ronnie glumly.

They each took a water bottle. Since Ronnie did not own one, he took one that Samuel provided. Samuel donned a wide-brimmed hat and clasped a carved hiking staff, looking like a heroic lead in an adventure film. He led the way to the trail.

Ronnie didn't know what was more monotonous, sitting at the campsite or walking through the woods. He stared at his feet, treading on the worn line of dirt so that he would not stumble over any ill-placed root or other object that could cause misfortune. Samuel scolded him with his lilting voice repeatedly that he was missing all the wonders that engulfed them. *It's a wonder my feet don't fall off.*

Samuel acted as tour guide, pointing out all the variety of trees, bushes, and vines that tore at Ronnie's clothes and scraped his tender skin. Meanwhile, they plodded forward. Ronnie counted his steps, though after five hundred, he gave up. And still they marched on. *The hobbits didn't walk this much.*

FWAP! A branch that Jerry pushed aside as he trudged down the trail swung back and walloped Ronnie in the face. He grabbed his nose, surprised that it didn't gush blood. "Watch it!"

"Serves you right for not looking where you're going," Jerry disgorged.

Trees. Oaks, maples, pines, birches. Each with different shaped leaves, with different textured barks, with different sized trunks. *Who cares? What does it matter? Cut them all down as far as I'm concerned. I want to get back home and play Skyrim.*

Ronnie lifted his foot to step over a stray fallen branch when the branch slithered forward. He screamed.

The other two spun around to see what caused his high-pitched panic.

"It's just a snake," Jerry hissed.

"It could've bitten me! I could've died!"

"It was just a grass snake. They don't have fangs. Stupid."

Samuel put a comforting hand on Ronnie's shoulder. "Are you okay? We can rest for a while."

"I'm fine." Ronnie was not about to let either of them know he was about to break out in tears. He stormed off down the trail, for once leading the way. Eventually, though, his slow pace caused the others to pass him, and again, he lagged behind.

Somehow, they had returned to camp. Ronnie couldn't remember turning around. Perhaps the trail was on a loop and brought them back to start. One thing was for sure, he would not ask and end up with a lecture on the geographic layout of the forest.

Lunch was simple cold cut sandwiches and chips. Ronnie devoured his food, feeling starved from the hike.

Afterward, Samuel and Jerry changed into swimsuits. Jerry snapped Ronnie with his towel. "Gonna join us or you gonna keep acting like a loser?"

Ronnie responded with a silent scowl.

Jerry shrugged. "Your loss."

Moments later, Ronnie heard splashes and hollers as his two companions enjoyed an apparently refreshing swim. He dug out a book and read several pages before feeling pangs of loneliness. *It's not fair that they're having fun and I'm miserable.*

He wandered down to the pond and brought his chair

this time so ants would not consume him. He watched as Samuel dove into the water, and then Jerry catapulted himself off the dock and folded his arms over his legs to perform a cannonball. An eruption of water caught Samuel off guard, and he dunked Jerry as he surfaced. Ronnie could not help but think that it looked fun and a tinge of regret surfaced that he had not brought a bathing suit. *The water's too cold*, he thought. *Though I really could use a bath after that hike. I'm covered with sweat and grime.*

As he experienced his friends' enjoyment vicariously, Ronnie again pondered why exactly he was out here. Those guys knew he did not want to camp—he never liked to go outside, let alone spend an entire weekend immersed in nature—and yet they persisted in pestering him until he relented. Did they just want to torment him? Perhaps Jerry, but not Samuel, who was too perfect to subject himself to such a petty endeavor. He truly wanted to spend his weekend with Ronnie, despite all his griping and sour attitude. Why?

Ronnie contemplated why he hung out with these guys at all. He had absolutely nothing in common with them. He met Jerry while working a college job at an electronics store. Jerry took an instant joy in tormenting him, though he brought Ronnie under his wing to teach him how to deal with customers. Social skills were not Ronnie's strength. After several months, Jerry convinced Ronnie to join him and his friends at a sports bar, despite that Ronnie hated sports and despised loud, crowded businesses. Before he knew it, Ronnie was spending much of his free time in Jerry's presence. Half of the time he tolerated it, while the rest was an endless source of annoyance.

Samuel entered the picture six months ago in one of the endless series of social gatherings that Jerry had dragged Ronnie to. Jerry and Samuel were opposites, yet they became fast friends. Ronnie put up with Jerry's barrage of insults, perhaps because he really thought that he deserved it, but Samuel's incessant benevolence confounded him. No one in the history of existence was that nice. Ronnie just could not wrap his mind around why either of them would be friends with him, and yet here the three were, spending a weekend away from all other humanity. It was surreal.

The afternoon wore on and the threesome found themselves back at camp lounging around, talking about completely inconsequential things. Ronnie actually took part in the conversation without complaining...much.

Dinner was superb yet deceptively simple—salmon fillets, a bag of mixed vegetables, and a bottle of ranch dressing tossed in together in a cast iron Dutch oven and set over the campfire for an hour. They wrapped aluminum foil around halved French bread covered with a thick salve of butter and garlic. The garlic bread toasted over the fire for a few minutes and came out with a light crunchy crust and a soft center that melted upon consuming. Fresh fruit slices completed the meal, which pleased Ronnie's taste buds.

The guitar came out again, and this time Ronnie actually allowed himself to enjoy the music. He surprised himself and others by actually joining in on the singing. His voice was fairly awful, but so was Jerry's. But it didn't matter because they were having fun.

Dessert was supposed to be what Samuel called dump cake. After cleaning out the Dutch oven, which was easy because it was a matter of pulling out the aluminum foil lining and wiping off the seasoned iron, Samuel poured cake mix, a can of fruit filling, and a stick of butter into the re-lined oven. It took close to an hour to cook in the fire with some hot coals resting on the lid. Samuel pulled it off the fire, opened the lid, and smiled as he saw with satisfaction that it turned out perfectly.

It was then that Jerry thought it would be funny to pick up Samuel's hiking staff and poke him in the ribs. Samuel jumped. The Dutch oven flew into the air. The dump cake splashed all over the ground. Jerry froze in mid-hyuck.

"What the hell did you do that for?" Samuel boomed.

"Damn, I'm so sorry," Jerry said, genuinely apologetic.

Samuel's face turned red. "There goes our dessert! God, I wish you'd grow up sometime."

"I didn't think you were gonna—"

"That's because you *never* think! You just act without using your brain! You call everyone else around you stupid, but you're the idiot!"

"It's just a stupid dump cake. It's not the end of the world."

Samuel got into Jerry's face. "*You* weren't the one who made it! *You* didn't buy the ingredients with your hard-earned money! *You* didn't go through the trouble of putting together this entire trip! *You* just went along for the ride and mooched off me, like you do with everyone!"

Jerry jabbed his knuckles into the approximation of where his hips should be. "At least I'm not a control freak like some people! I wanted to go some place with chicks, but noooo...we had to come out into the middle of nowhere because you wanted to be one with nature."

Ronnie watched the escalation with huge, round eyes

that threatened to pop out of his skull. He forced his breath into his lungs. His heart raced. The scene playing out before him terrified him, as he had never seen these two fight before—in fact, this was the first time he had ever seen Samuel lose his cool. Ronnie could not deal with this.

"STOP IT!"

Their faces a mere inch from each other, Samuel and Jerry both stopped in mid-yell and turned to Ronnie.

"What's wrong with you two?" Ronnie pleaded. "Want to ruin a great night over a stupid cake? You were having so much fun fishing and hiking and swimming and singing. What happened? You can't just throw it all away like this. You guys are best friends. You don't want to hurt each other. Come on."

Tempers defused, the two combatants could do nothing except look abashedly at the ground.

"It was just a stupid cake," Samuel said.

"What I did was pretty lame," Jerry added.

Samuel gazed heavenward. "Look at those stars. Makes me feel inconsequential."

Ronnie tilted his head up and immediately felt an overwhelming sensation of vertigo. Billions of bright pinpoints shined down on him. He always thought that *Star Trek* and *Star Wars* overdid it with the stars in the scenes where ships sped through space. He now realized that those movies underestimated the awesomeness of a clear, cloudless night sky.

"Wow," he said. It was the only thing he could think of to express the strange mixture of emotions that coursed through his soul at that moment.

WHEN RONNIE HIT THE SACK THAT NIGHT, HE EXPECTED ANOTHER round of sleeplessness, but as soon as his head touched his pillow, he was out. Morning arrived unexpectedly, and he awoke as the dawn lit up his tent. His muscles were sore, but he was oddly refreshed.

The others were still asleep when he crawled out of his tent, so he strolled down to the pond and sat on the end of the dock with his bare feet dangling into the water. He enjoyed the cool feel as he wiggled his toes. He could not remember any time previously in his life when he was more at peace.

Upon hearing the others stirring, he returned to camp. They had a light breakfast of cereal before packing up the campsite. Ronnie had to have help to take down his tent, but he paid attention to the procedure and noted all the pieces of the assembly so that next time, he could manage solo.

They brought all the gear to the truck and then Samuel handed Jerry the items for him to pack in the bed. He had a system, so it was best for Ronnie to stay out of the way.

Ronnie ambled down the trail and looked around at the foliage. It was really amazing how many types of plants cohabitated in such a small area. He reached down and plucked a leaf from a vine and examined it. The almond-shaped leaf had an interesting reddish hue to its overall dark green coloration. He noted with interest that the leaves grew in groups of three—just like he and his two buddies. He picked the other two leaves that were clumped together with the one in his hand, and for good luck put them in his pocket.

I think I'll remember this trip for a long time.

NEVER FORGET

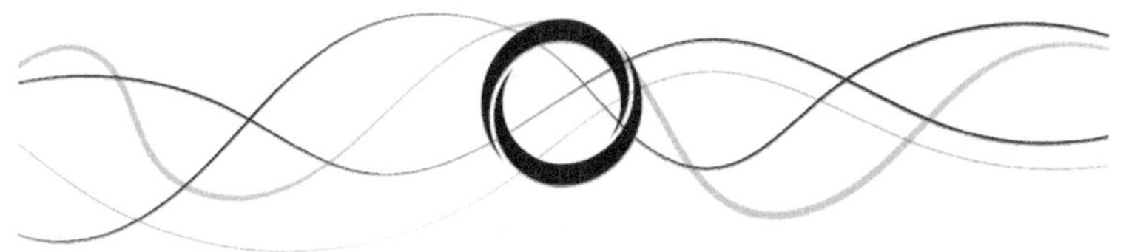

On that beautiful, sunny, terrible day
When the smoke rose into the sky and the cloud
    filled the streets,
On the gray, bleak days that followed
We were told to repeat
Never forget, never forget.

We watched as they died, inside we died as well.
We waited under the silent skies, wondering
    what was next,
Filled with horror, hatred, despair.
How do we go on?
Never forget, never forget.
I want to forget.

Complacency replaced with paranoia,
Liberties with patriotism, The War on Drugs
*   with The War on Terror.*
We were a country united,
All soon divided.
Never forget, never forget.
I want to forget.

We witnessed tragedy at the hands of Man,
Yet we still fall to the mercy of Mother Nature.
The Towers fell, the levees too.
The blame thrown around.
Never forget, never forget.
I want to forget.

Change is inevitable; you can't stop it.
Like a boy becoming a man, still the same yet
*   different.*
A strange resemblance of the past.
Do we want the past?
Never forget, never forget.
I want to forget.

There's no way to predict what is yet to come
Due to human frailty or because of an act of God.
To honor those who've perished
Live to the fullest.
Never forget, never forget.
I will never forget.

○

A SNOWBALL'S CHANCE

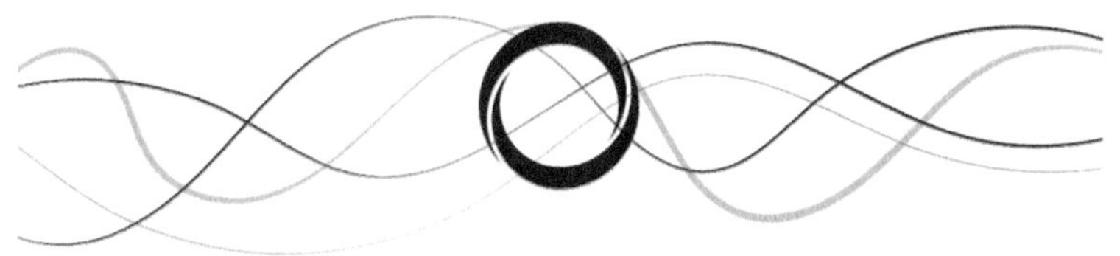

Tiny crystals in the newly fallen snow glistened in the bright sun, making the white blanket a giant reflector inlaid with millions of microscopic mirrors that blinded me as I trudged across my front yard. My moon boots crunched through the crusty top layer of snow, leaving a trail of foot-shaped indentions behind me. Icy breath burned my trachea even though I wore a woolen scarf tied around my face as if I were a well-padded bandit. The air had a preternatural stillness to it that only fresh snowfall generates. All the sounds seemed muffled, as if noise-reduction padding layered the Earth.

I approached the old apple tree, which had several boards nailed to its outstretched limbs that served as a fort, and continued on until I reached the edge of the cliff. I almost missed it because of the snowdrift, but my insulated foot found the boundary where solid ground disappeared.

Had I overstepped, all that would have happened would have been me sinking down a few inches into the hard-packed mass along the hillside.

My house, a two-story brick-faced Colonial with enough room to hold my parents, my four siblings, and me in comfort, sat at the top of a hill amid several acres of land. A horse pasture consumed half of it with a barn in the back of the property. Sprawling farms had once filled the township of Water Mill, Michigan, but farmers had sold off chunks of their land to factory workers who moved out of Detroit in order to raise their kids in the countryside with room to roam. Mine was such a family.

From my perch, I saw my dad's car turn the corner a quarter of a mile away and head for the house. Chippewa Lane was a dirt road that dead ended far into the woods and was barely wide enough for two cars to pass without knocking off their side mirrors. Whoever had excavated the road had cut through our hill as it sloped upward, making a gradually growing wall of dirt that rose from the roadside. At its peak, this cliff was perhaps twelve feet tall, though to my nine-year-old self, it seemed like the face of a mountain. In the winter, wind blew snow off the drop-off, where the powder drifted across the road. Some kind neighbor would attach a blade to his pickup truck and plow a single lane on the far side, leaving a deep embankment for us kids to enjoy.

My dad's Mercury inched along over the ice-covered sand and gravel and then passed underneath me. I waved, but if my dad saw me, he paid no attention. Keeping the vehicle from sliding into the snowbank was more important than acknowledging his son. He reached the driveway, which spiraled up and around the hill and ended at the cement parking space in front of the garage. The car made it a few feet before the tires spun, losing purchase. This was typical. True to form, my dad put the car in reverse and backed across the road and down my neighbor's driveway that opened directly across from our own. The house was set deep in the property at the base of a little valley filled with bare pear trees. Its driveway was long and straight, perfect to use as a launching pad to bring a car to top speed and propel it up the arc of our own driveway. It was scary riding in the car when my dad did this, but it was exciting to watch from a distance. His car raced toward our property, zipped across the frozen dirt lane without slowing—fortunately there was no oncoming traffic—and fishtailed around the sloped curve to finish successfully in his parking spot.

I waved again as my dad got out of the car. He still took no notice of me and went inside. He must have wanted to get into the warmth of the house.

With no cars coming down the road, it was safe to play in the snowbank. I leaped. The thrill of plummeting through the air lasted a mere second, but it seemed to stretch indefinitely. Then I plunged into the drift and sank to my waist. In the summer, this would have been suicidal; but in the winter, I had the cushion of the snow to break my fall.

A heavy storm had dumped a ton of frozen precipitation on us that obliterated the road and left us and all the neighbors landlocked until someone could clear a lane. The blizzard was a source of frustration and anxiety for adults, but for the kids, it was a reason for celebration—no school! The snow gave us countless forms of entertainment—building snowmen, having intense snowball fights, and sledding down the hill and underneath the strands of barbed wire fence at the base without getting snagged on the rusty points.

The one activity that my friends and I preferred over all others was to dig tunnels through the snowdrift against the cliff. It started with us hollowing out caves, but when we realized the ceilings did not collapse on us, we mined deeper like dogs paddling out a cloud of debris behind us. The tunnels snaked through the drift, from the ground up to the top of the hillside, running the length of the dirt wall the snow lay against. A dozen openings at various places linked with secret passages. We spent hours crawling through the hidden network, sometimes on our hands and knees, sometimes shimmying on our bellies. It was a special place that only belonged to the children of our country neighborhood. I don't think any of our parents even knew about it; I certainly never said a word.

When the digging was done and we grew bored with just hanging out in the tunnels, war broke out. Each one of us claimed an aperture and fortified our base with as many snowballs as we could make with our glove-covered hands. Someone counted down, and then the battle began. We threw the snowballs at each other with as much might as our arms clad in downy coats or snowmobile suits allowed. The padding helped shield us from the force of the snow-balls pounding us, at least when the frozen projectiles actu-ally hit their targets. We ducked into the tunnels for shelter and to re-arm ourselves with more ammunition. These conflicts raged on until we were exhausted, then we returned to hanging out in our glacial hideaway.

Sunset came early in those wintry days. It was never a problem staying out after it got dark, as long as I came in for supper after my dad got home from work. His was usually one of the last of a long stream of cars that crept up the slippery, ice-covered road to pass us in our fortress that was virtually invisible in the dark.

My best friend, Jack, was a punk. There's really no other way to say it. He was a scrawny little kid who was the same size as me despite being three years older. Being the youngest in a family of eight, he endured bullying by his four brothers and dished it out on the younger kids in the neighborhood. He was obnoxious, demanding, vulgar, and an all-around twerp—yet I hung out with him nearly constantly. Maybe his bad boy behavior was an attraction, since I was just the opposite. I was incapable of imagining any of the mischievous and often downright mean things he dreamed up, some of which he talked me into doing. One such activity was to throw snowballs at the cars that drove past after darkness fell.

It sounded like fun.

We hid in our tunnel entrances when a car turned onto Chippewa Lane. As it approached, we knew the driver could only see what the twin beams from the car's headlights lit directly in front of it. We prepared our round missiles and then dropped out of sight. The sound of the approaching car grew loud in the still air. The smell of exhaust filled our hiding holes. We sensed our quarry next to us. It was now or never. In one swift movement, all of us popped up out of our holes like prairie dogs and pelted the moving vehicle with every snowball in our possession. White splatters burst across the side of the car. Within seconds, the assault ended, and we vanished from sight. The car slowed to a stop past our driveway and the driver emerged to investigate what made those horrible thumping noises. Upon finding no damage other than the smattering of frosty explosions across the car's hull, he climbed back inside and drove away. Of course, there was no sign of the perpetrators.

That scenario played out dozens more times, night after night. We were never caught.

As with everything when young, repeated activities grow tiresome after a short while. Kids need new stimuli to hold their attention. We eventually drifted away from the tunnels, which shrank as snow melted and refroze.

One night as winter dragged on, I hung out with Jack and his brother Jerry, who was a year older than him and had become tall and gangly with the onset of adolescence. We wandered down the road to the primary thoroughfare, another dirt road that was much wider and better maintained than the one we lived on. Being a mischievous brat, Jack suggested ambushing the next car that came along. Jack and I stayed on the side of the road closest to our houses, positioning ourselves between a wooden fence and the mound of dirty plowed snow piled along the shoulder of the road. Jerry concealed himself on the far side so we could hit the vehicle from both fronts. We made a dozen snowballs apiece.

The wait seemed to take forever, though in reality it was probably all of about ten minutes. We saw headlights crest a distant hill. We readied ourselves for attack. The thrill of the secretive fight excited us. Finally, a small, white four-door car drove past, its occupants unaware of the trap we had set.

WHUMP! WHUMP! WHUMP!

Our ammo hit its mark. We disappeared like ninjas.

The car reached the corner and stopped. That itself was

not a concern, because we had seen that happen repeatedly. Several people got out, which also was not unusual. Voices drifted to us. We remained still as prone statues to avoid being detected. The driver and passengers climbed back into the car. We heard its engine rev, but the car did not move. Angry shouts echoed down the tree-lined alley to us. This was new—every other time, the car drove away without incident. What had changed?

"Let's get out of here." An edge of panicked urgency sliced Jack's whispered, high-pitched voice. Without waiting for a response, he rolled under a wooden slat on the fence. I followed his lead and found myself in a horse pasture. Jack had already taken off running, leaving me to fend for myself. I trailed behind, but could not run as fast as Jack. I might have been the same size as him, but he still had three years of muscle development ahead of me.

I looked back at the road. Silhouetted figures milled around the spot we had just vacated. Deep voices roared. I could not make out the words, but the tone showed that they had found Jerry. My imagination ran wild with possibilities of what these mysterious men were doing to the poor kid who had no chance of escape.

My legs pumped faster, but the snow became deeper the further I progressed into the field that sloped upward toward the owner's house. My diminutive body grew tired. Sanctuary was too far away. I would not make it. I had to hide and take my chances.

I swerved to the side of the pasture and dropped flat against the fence, hoping that it would be enough to conceal me. It wasn't.

Within minutes, those shadowy people from the car

descended upon me—four impossibly tall, demon-like creatures stretched beyond recognition as human. They all spoke at once in a cacophony of violent words, screaming filthy language that was impossible for me to assimilate. All I knew was that these guys were filled with venom. I shook with terror, knowing that I would not survive this encounter.

"Where do you live?" one of behemoths questioned. His tone of voice penetrated my shell of fear. I realized that these monstrous beings were teenagers, perhaps college age. Their fury radiated off them like a nuclear blast. I needed to answer their question, lest I suffer from whatever physical torture they could inflict on me. I couldn't find my voice, so I just pointed—to a random house that was not my own. This seemed to satisfy them, and they departed.

I lay still, recovering from that close call with death. I breathed hard. My pulse raced. I sweated inside my bundle of clothing that protected me from the frigid temperature. Finally, I calmed down enough to climb to my feet and plod back home.

Entering my house, I stripped off my cold-weather outerwear. My socks had slid down my feet and had gathered at my toes. I walked past my dad, who was stretched out on the couch, engaged in a news broadcast. He took no notice of me as I warmed myself by the fireplace.

After thawing out, I called Jack on the phone that was connected to the wall in the kitchen. "What happened to you?" he queried. He truly sounded concerned. "I booked it on home."

I described my ordeal.

"Jerry got home a few minutes ago," he explained. "They got to him and screamed and cussed at him."

"Did they hurt him?"

"Naw. He's okay." Jack sounded disappointed.

The next day, the three of us got together and repeated our adventures to each other, making it sound more exciting with each telling. We meandered to the house on the corner, where two brothers younger than me lived. We didn't really like the Mallory boys much, but it was a place to congregate.

Their father came out and spoke to us. "Were you guys out here last night?"

Fear stabbed us in the spine. "No," we all muttered. "Why?"

"It seems that some kids were throwing snowballs at cars."

Uh-oh.

"One stopped in front of the house. The guys in it thought something was wrong with their car, so they got out to look. The passenger door got caught in the snowbank. In order to pull it loose, they decided to rock the car. When they did, the door ripped off its hinges."

Our mouths dropped open. No wonder those guys were so furious.

Mr. Malllory eyed us suspiciously. "Sure you don't know anything about that?"

We shook our heads. "We had nothing to do with that," Jack said with a straight face. I'm sure mine was plastered with guilt. My mind conjured the image of those guys driving home with the door crammed in the back seat, with the icy wind blowing in through the open doorway. We were lucky to have not been killed.

Jack, Jerry, and I made an excuse to leave. We managed to barely step foot off their property before bursting out laughing, both at the ridiculous situation of a car door wedged in the embankment and at our narrow escape from death.

We never threw snowballs at cars again.

LAST STAND AT THE BELLMONT MISSION

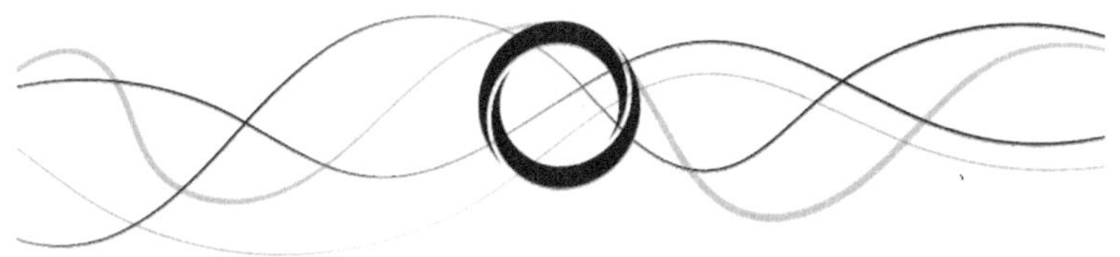

1

The wind whistled through the bell tower with a ghostly howl. The coarse grains of sand scraped against the weathered walls, etching away the cracked paint.

Morgan pulled himself slowly up the narrow staircase, step by step, his all but useless legs dragging behind. He didn't feel the slivers of wood embed themselves into his flesh.

The thought of the buzzard filled his mind like a ghastly vision. The bird had followed him for days, circling above, gliding on currents of air with wings spread in an almost relaxed pose, waiting for Morgan to finally collapse and take his dying breath. But Morgan got the better of it. He was in shelter now, and the bird would have to work a little harder for the bits of meat still left on his bones.

He knew the bird would find him eventually.

A wooden plank covered the top of the stairs. Although it was a mere flimsy covering intended to keep out the elements, Morgan could barely lift it and push it aside.

He was a determined man. His determination kept him alive this long, although it was also his undoing. That same determination brought him to the uppermost part of the tower, the open balcony where the huge bell hung. This was a safe place, at least as safe as he could find. It also gave him the advantage of seeing in all directions. They would come, eventually, and he wanted to be ready for them.

The desert spread out as far as he could see, everywhere he looked. The brown, desolate wasteland seemed to mock him. It knew that he temporarily escaped its harshness, but it would win in the end. It could wait. It had all the time in the world.

A gust of wind blew through the tower. The bell, looking so ancient and forgotten, swung on its near-frozen joint. It rang out weakly, a mere memory of the majesty that it once sang.

Morgan wondered if his bones would be found up here one day, as dry and weathered as the mission itself, a virtual part of the building, long dead.

Heat waves rose from the earth in the distance. Morgan stared in that direction, expecting men on horses to ride out of the distortion. But no riders came, only sand.

He couldn't remember from which direction he had staggered and could barely remember that act. He knew it could not have been very long ago, for his body could not last very long. Regardless, the memory seemed distant, as if being recalled from childhood. In that fractured recollection, he saw himself as if from someone else's eyes. In fact, he felt rather detached from himself now and wondered if perhaps he was dead already.

He had been riding hard, he knew, trying to put as much ground between himself and his pursuers. He had hoped to throw them off in the desert, to lead them out, then double back around. Unfortunately, his plan backfired and he found himself lost in the scorched plain.

The realization of the foolishness of his plan came all too late. His followers would not have been tricked by such an immature plan. They were expert trackers and would hunt him down no matter where he went. They would eventually find him here. He just hoped he could last long enough to see their shocked faces when they faced the living corpse and found a few surprises left in him.

The revolver felt heavy in his hand, but it was a comforting weight. Four bullets rested in the chambers, awaiting their duty. One was for him. After all of this, he was still going to make the final decision in his life. Another bullet was for Petrie. The remaining two were for whoever was standing nearby. He couldn't get them all, but he was going to take as many with him as he could.

He scouted a dark spot silhouetted against the bright sky. The bird had returned. Perhaps he would use one of the bullets on it. He wondered how buzzard tasted. The thought of feeding on the scavenger struck him as ironic and he let out a hoarse bark of a laugh. The sound was alien to him.

Morgan's steed had died days ago, the heat and strain finally getting the best of it. His supply of food and water was limited, and it did not last long after his companion had fallen. He wandered through the desert, baking under the intense sun. For the longest time, he could think of nothing else but food and water. Later, his mind drifted and he could not keep a coherent thought for long before it dissipated into meaningless images.

His stomach contracted, constantly screaming to be filled. His tongue swelled and became dry, leathery, as if he had swallowed an old shoe. Tear ducts evaporated, leaving his eyes scratchy and painful. His arms and face cracked and peeled with sunburn while his feet calloused and bled.

The mission had appeared before him like a miracle, a spectral image of salvation, a white castle rising out of the dust and reaching toward heaven. His hopes soared, although he knew it must be a mirage.

The mission unwavered before him as he approached, rather than dissipating before his eyes into the sandy heat distortion. Disappointment settled in when he saw it had long since been deserted. It was yet another corpse lying in the desert sun.

A sign near the entrance proclaimed it "Bellmont Mission, by the grace of God." The worn letters were mere ghosts of a previous existence. Morgan wondered how long it had been since anyone had worshipped within these walls. It didn't matter. If nothing else, this mission served the purpose of giving a beaten man one last chance at redemption.

2

The world was dark and cold. Morgan realized this state suddenly, disoriented by the unfamiliarity of the surroundings. He slowly realized where he was and remembered how he had gotten there.

It was night. He must have slipped into sleep without knowing it. This had happened to him several times while wandering the desert, although he probably couldn't call it sleeping. The world would drift away into a numb abyss, then he would walk through some unfamiliar terrain and realize that he had not been conscious of his actions for some time. Those blackouts occurred randomly and unexpectedly and it scared him, though he was now grateful to be spared experiencing every minute of the ordeal of his journey.

He was hungry again. He considered it a good sign, since he had felt nothing for the longest time.

His mind was clearer and sharper. He could think more rationally.

It was amazing what some sheltered sleep could do.

He thought out his situation. It was still very bleak, but a sliver of hope had worked its way into the picture. Perhaps some small animals made the mission their home. Morgan could feed on them. Even if his pursuers did not follow him this far, it was likely that some travelers would pass by. There had to have been some route to the mission when it was operational. Chances were that the hypothetical road was still in use.

People had once lived there. That meant that water must have been available, at least at one time. If the mission had closed down because the well had dried up, perhaps water had since returned..

Morgan's hopes were running high, and he was actually in good spirits. He might just make it out of this after all.

Tomorrow he must explore the building. He might find other things he didn't expect.

He decided he needed to rest. When he closed his eyes again, sleep claimed him, taking him to the peaceful recesses of his soul.

3

With the sunrise, the heat soon became overbearing and he could not sleep any longer. He felt surprisingly refreshed.

His legs were still very stiff and troublesome, but he moved around better than the night before. A long, straight branch of deadwood served as a staff.

The mission seemed even more desolate in the daylight, since Morgan could now see precisely the decrepit state in which it existed. The interior walls had all but fallen, the wood rotted and the stone crumbled. Holes in the walls and ceiling let in broken splotches of sunlight. Sand had collected in tiny dunes in every spot the wind could carry it.

Food was nonexistent. Several bags with ragged holes torn in the bottoms lay scattered about what Morgan assumed were the pantry and kitchen areas. Small animals must have been in here at one time, although they might have disappeared with the food supply.

The well was in a tiny courtyard outside the kitchen. It was a simple hole in the ground, supported by bricks. The wooden cross-beam had fallen over the opening and a frayed rope hung from it. Morgan pulled up the rope and found a bucket tied at its end. Dry sand filled the pail, but moisture caked its bottom. Water was down there, but it would take some work to get to it.

Morgan examined the hole and calculated that it was large enough for him to squeeze through. He pulled the crossbeam aside and tied the rope around his waist. He hoped it was strong enough to hold his weight. If it broke, he didn't think he could climb back out.

Morgan stood over the hole for a long while, deliberating. He was no coward, but events of the past several days made him wary. He was likely to die shortly, but he didn't want to give up. If an accident were to occur, he would surely die. If he did not get water soon, he would definitely die.

Dangling his legs over the precipice, Morgan took a tight hold on the rope and slid into the well. He scraped the sides, kicking dirt down before him.

Darkness engulfed Morgan, the harsh light from the circle above absorbed by the dust in the air. The atmosphere in the shaft was refreshingly cool and clammy, but the sensation of being swallowed by the earth overcame him.

He stopped, his weary muscles tiring rapidly.

The rope was holding, but for how long?

He started again, letting out bits of the rope at a time. His hands were in pain from rope burn, but he couldn't afford to think about it.

After an eternity, his feet touched the ground. He released the rope and leaned back with relief against the dirt wall. He looked up.

The bright circle of the mouth of the well was tiny, far away. The tightness and closeness surrounding Morgan again seized him, squeezing him. Feeling around in the dark, he discovered there was nowhere to go but up. There was no other passage down here, just the walls and the floor. It was a deep cylinder, and the top was high over his head.

Morgan choked down the panic, but it stayed close to the surface. He couldn't let it get the best of him and had to press on. The quicker he gathered water, the sooner he could get out of here. Assuming, of course, that he had the strength to climb out.

Drawing himself up tightly, Morgan slowly slid into a crouch. He maneuvered the bucket, still tied to the end of the rope, out from underneath himself. He felt the ground. It was damp. He wasn't going to acquire much water, but any bit would do.

He dug his fingers into the moist soil, pulling up a hand-ful. He held it over the bucket and squeezed with all his dwindled strength. A few drops of water fell from his hand, making tinny plunking noises in the pail.

He repeated this procedure, soon digging out a bowl in the dirt. Water collected there, which Morgan could cup out with his hand. Soiled water soon covered the bottom of the bucket.

He scooped out some water and brought it to his lips. It was dirty and gritty, but it tasted marvelous to his parched mouth. His tongue soaked it in greedily, and he drank more and more, trying to quench his tremendous thirst that had now reawakened.

He did not know how long he stayed down there, but he had grown tired and his fingers hurt. He had collected a good amount of water that, if doled out properly, might last him a few days.

Turning to the task of climbing out of the well, he tested

the rope and dragged his weight back up. This was much more difficult, but he found he could use his knees as support. The bucket trailed underneath him and he was careful not to make it rock so none of the precious water would spill out.

He reached out of the opening and grasped the wooden support brace, then pulled himself into the open air. Although much hotter than inside the hole, it was fresh and clean, and he breathed deeply.

The daylight had diminished. The sun had already set beyond the far horizon, leaving discolored streaks of red and orange like flames drifting from the earth. He didn't realize he had been down there all day, but felt ready for a rest.

4

Morgan slept in the bell tower again that night. In one room he explored, he found a bed with a mattress that was still fairly well held together, but he did not feel comfortable there, so he elected to return to the tower.

A cool breeze wafted over him like a pleasant dream. He held the bucket of water next to him tightly like the treasure that it was.

He slept.

5

Day arrived all too soon.

Several tiny insects had gathered around the water. Morgan couldn't figure out how they found him or where they came from, but he didn't care. He swatted them and ate them. Miniscule protein was better than none.

He looked out over the landscape. It was the same, always the same.

He promised himself that if he made it out of the desert alive, he would go somewhere wet, with lots of vegetation.

He drew a swallow of water and savored it. His mouth demanded more, more, but he refrained. To give in would mean giving up, and giving up was one thing he would not do.

Something caught his eye, and at first he thought it was just a trick of the sunlight. He squinted and looked hard to the southeast and saw it.

A black shape moved on the horizon. As he watched, he realized it was several shapes moving toward him.

They had found him at last.

His breath grew shallow, and his heartbeat raced. He crouched down in hiding, finding a crack in the wood, which allowed him to spy at the approaching figures.

The rational part of his mind assured him that the people could be anybody, simple travelers passing by. In fact, this could be his salvation.

His gut told him something different. Instinctively, he knew it was Petrie and his hired guns, finally tracking him down.

6

Petrie squinted at the mission. The state of decay in which the mission existed disgusted him. He was not a religious man, but he was civilized.

"Search it," he said to his four companions. Two of them, Crowe and Haynes, had been with him from the outset, had in fact been working for him for some time now. The other two, Mikenson and Yute, had joined him in the last city he traveled through. Morgan had a way of forcing him to hire new guns often. The newcomers had no commitment in finding Morgan other than their pay, but Petrie's long-time accomplices had a personal stake in the matter. They had watched several of their friends die at the hands of the fugitive.

The men dismounted and separated, each taking a different section of the mission. Petrie remained on his horse. It was a long shot that Morgan had survived long enough to reach this place, but they had found no body in the desert. His men were experts. If there were a body, they would have found it.

One look at the deserted buildings and Petrie knew the outlaw was here. It was now just a matter of finding him.

He had lost too much to let Morgan live.

7

Crowe stepped cautiously down the upstairs hall in the main building. There was no telling if the floor would give way at any minute. Rays of sun sifted through the holes in the ceiling, particles of dust dancing in the beams.

He had his revolver drawn, anticipating the worse. The newly hired guns thought it was foolish to think the fugitive would be here, but Petrie believe it so Crowe believed it, too.

He had seen Morgan slip out of tight situations before, and there was no reason to think his luck was changing.

If Morgan were here, Crowe would not let him take him by surprise. He was tricky, and Crowe had seen several of his buddies die from those tricks.

8

Mikenson walked up the creaky steps of the bell tower. He thought this was foolish, but went along with it, anyway. The pay was very good. He just hoped Petrie would keep his end of the bargain. He had only recently joined the party but had Petrie figured out as someone who would stab his own mother in the back if it were profitable.

He passed a small window whose glass had long since been busted out. He could not see Petrie, who was on the other side of the tower. The main building lay about twenty feet below.

Reaching the top of the stairs, Mikenson threw aside the board covering the entrance to the platform and aimed his pistol about, just in case someone was up here. His earlier suspicions were correct. The platform was empty.

Holstering his gun, he pulled himself up to look around. Previously, he had only gone as high as a second floor, so this was quite a shock for him. It was very high and he felt a little dizzy.

There was no reason to stay up here any longer, so he turned to climb back down but noticed a bucket in the corner partially filled with water. The water did not look septic, as if it had been sitting for a long time. In fact, it looked quite fresh, if not a little muddy. He poked two fingers into the water, then stuck them in his mouth. Sure enough, the water tasted fine.

Someone had been up here, and recently.

He turned back to the railing to call out to Petrie, who needed to be alerted immediately. Petrie was partially hidden behind a building. Mikenson cupped his mouth with his hands and took a deep breath, but a shape dropped in front of him and crashed into his stomach. He was propelled backwards and fell into a heap inches from the gaping stairwell.

Rage swelled in him, and he didn't even think to draw his gun.

9

Morgan picked himself up quickly from where he dropped. He had shimmied onto the roof when he heard Mikenson approaching and could see down at him through the cracks in the roof. He knew that if he let the man call out to Petrie, he would be trapped, so he had to think fast. The only thing he could do was to swing down and kick Mikenson away from the railing. It was chancy, but it succeeded, so far.

Only now he faced the rather large man angrily charging him.

With the bucket of water still fresh on his mind, he grabbed for it and threw the water in Mikenson's face just before the man crashed into him. Mikenson stopped and clawed at his eyes, which were now filled with the dirty water. Morgan used that brief reprieve to swing the bucket in an arc and catch Mikenson across the back of the head. The hired gun stumbled forward and fell against the railing, where gravity took hold and toppled him over.

Morgan took a quick glance over the edge in time to see Mikenson hit the hard-packed dirt at the base of the tower. He ducked down just as Petrie came into view to see what had happened.

Petrie now knew Morgan was here. He could not remain hidden any longer. He just hoped he could last long enough to take Petrie with him.

He dropped into the stairwell and hurried down the steps as quickly as he could. Adrenaline was pumping through his veins now, so he had more energy than he had in many days.

Already he could hear Petrie's voice calling out to the rest of his men, ordering them to rush to the bell tower.

Morgan did not have enough time. There was no way he could leave the tower and not be seen. He was defenseless and trapped.

He passed the window and paused. He could drop to the roof below, but that wasn't a guaranteed escape. If he had been in better condition, he wouldn't have thought twice about it, but being in his current state made him wary. But there was no other choice.

Pulling himself onto the sill, he swung his legs through and pushed off. The drop was quick, and he readied himself for the impact.

He hit.

The sound of wood breaking filled his ears, almost drowning out the sound of bone breaking.

10

Petrie looked down at the dead man. This was becoming a habit, but one that was soon ending.

His head spun up at the sound of the crash, like a bird dog spotting a grouse. The game was reaching a conclusion, and the outcome was a sure thing.

11

Crowe slowly realized that he was hearing Petrie shouting. He was at the far end of the wing, in a large room filled with skeletons of beds. He guessed that this was an orphanage or a sick ward. The wind was howling through the cracks in the walls, making a hollow, haunting whine.

Upon deciphering Petrie's voice, he rushed back down the hall when the ceiling exploded before him. He dove out of the way just as the wooden beam from above splintered to the floor. A man fell through, collapsing in a heap. Crowe took delight in recognizing Morgan.

He stood and stepped next to the prone man, who was breathing shallowly, a trickle of blood dribbling from the corner of his mouth.

"All this time searching for you, and you just fall at my feet," Crowe chuckled.

Morgan's eyes fluttered open and he looked up at Crowe blankly.

Crowe pulled back a foot, preparing to kick Morgan across the face. Morgan's quick movement amazed Crowe during the instant before the board slammed into his knees. Crowe dropped to the floor with a yelp of pain and immediately felt his face sear with pain. Consciousness left him in a swirl of lights and colors.

12

The board fell to the floor next to Crowe. Morgan grasped the revolver, which was still clutched in Crowe's hand, and crawled away from the scene of violence. His left leg was numb and twisted oddly. He didn't want to look at it, but through his peripheral vision, his foot appeared to be facing behind him. Scratches and cuts slashed across his arms, and he was having a hard time breathing. He was losing a lot of blood from several places. His abdomen felt as if it were on fire.

His physical ailments were not important right now. He had to find a hiding spot. He was in pain and needed serious medical treatment, but first he had to survive Petrie. At least now he had a fighting chance.

13

Petrie smashed a board into the wall, creating yet another hole. His two remaining men stood gawking at him.

"What are you waiting for?" he screamed at them. "Find them! How hard can that be?" He pointed at the trail of blood that led down the hall.

Haynes and Yute scrambled away from their boss, in as much a hurry to leave the vicinity of Petrie's wrath as to find Morgan.

Another casualty. Although Crowe was still living, he

was useless now. His jaw had been shattered, and he would probably remain unconscious for hours.

More than anything else, Petrie needed to see Morgan dead.

14

The trail of blood led into the far room that was the bed tomb, and disappeared through a man-sized hole in the wall in the corner.

"You follow the trail," Haynes told Yute. "I'll corner him from the other side. He can't be too far." With that, Haynes rushed out of the room.

Yute, who was the youngest of the group, ducked through the hole. He found himself in another room that was in worse shape than the one he left. The trail of blood was spotty, so Morgan may have been able to slow its flow, but it was still evident. There were tracks in the dust from where the wounded man must have dragged himself across the floor. Yute grinned. Tracking him was going to be easier than he thought.

The trail led him into another hallway, where the blood ended at a smallish hole in the floorboards. Haynes had not made it here yet, so Yute continued to follow Morgan. Finding the fugitive would please Petrie, who might just give him a good-sized bonus.

He dropped through the hole and landed in a parlor of some sorts on the first floor. The blood was gone, but the track in the dirt was still quite visible. It went through yet another crevice in a wall.

This was becoming tiresome. Morgan couldn't have

much energy after losing all that blood. Eventually, his body would give out. This was just making it easier for Yute.

He crawled through this hole, which took him into a dark, cramped closet. His eyes slowly adjusted to the light and he made out his surroundings. The outline of a man came into focus, but before he could fire, there was an explosion of flames and he felt no more.

15

Morgan looked into the face of the dead young man and felt remorse. He took the life of someone who never started down the right path, and now would never get the chance.

He reminded himself that this was a matter of survival and he needed to do whatever it took to live.

From what he could tell, there was now only one more hired gun besides Petrie himself to deal with. The odds were better, but not terrific.

16

Petrie winced at the sound of the gunshot. Instinctively, he knew who had fired the gun, and also knew that the bullet had found its mark.

He turned and calmly walked back down the steps.

17

Haynes raced toward the sound of the gunshot. It came from the first floor, but in his rush he got confused and could not remember where the sound came from. He searched through all the rooms, angry at himself for getting flustered. Like Petrie, he too knew the source of the gunshot and its target.

He walked into the kitchen, nerves on edge. Even though Morgan was wounded and possibly dying, he was still dangerous. He knew that all too well from experience. The events of the past few minutes proved that.

His heart seemed to miss a beat as he caught sight of Morgan's telltale crawl track. It led from the far doorway directly to a closed closet door.

Taking a deep breath to calm himself, Haynes turned to begin his search once again, but a familiar click made him stop dead in his tracks.

"Wouldn't shoot a man when he isn't looking, would ya?" Haynes asked to the man he could not yet see.

"Wouldn't shoot a crippled man, would ya?" Morgan retorted. His voice was strained, full of pain. "I'd drop the gun, if I was you."

Haynes let the revolver slip from his fingers. It dropped to the floor with a wooden thud. He slowly turned to face Morgan with mild surprise at what he saw.

The fugitive was propped against the doorjamb, a frayed board shoved under his armpit for support. Blood, mud, and sweat streaked him. He was very pale and skinny, with hollow circles under his eyes. His cheekbones protruded over his sunken cheeks. One leg was twisted at an inhuman angle. The hand that held the gun was rock solid.

"It's good to see you're in such a good health," Haynes said. Although he put on a cocky mannerism, although Morgan was in terrible condition, he still feared the gunbearer and he knew he could lose his life in an instant if he wasn't careful.

"Call Petrie."

"I don't think I should do that."

"As you pointed out, my health is on somewhat shaky grounds. My finger could twitch uncontrollably at any moment. Call Petrie."

"Petrie!"

"I am here," replied Petrie's calm voice from the other doorway. He stepped in, weapon holstered, arms crossed.

"It's ending now," said Morgan.

"I agree," said Petrie, and he turned and walked out.

"Wait!" Morgan yelled, confused.

"Shoot him if you like, Morgan," Petrie called from down the hall. "I'll hire another."

"Where are you going?!"

"Outside. I have all the time in the world. Unfortunately, you don't." His footsteps faded away, and with a bang of a door, Morgan knew he was outside.

"He's right, you know," Haynes said, grinning. "You're gonna die. Pretty soon now, as far as I can see."

He took a step toward Morgan.

"All he has to do is wait…"

Another step.

"…and you'll drop dead."

He was very close now.

"And he can just carry your body back home…"

He was face to face with him.

"…and prove to Caroline who's the best man."

With Haynes's words, Morgan felt himself boil with confusion and hurt and anger. What was he supposed to do?

Petrie was right. He was going to drop dead soon. And there was nothing he could do about it. But the thought of his dear Caroline becoming even more victimized than she had been—to be put through the torment of seeing the corpse of her true love paraded before her as a trophy from a spurned lover—was too much for him to take.

He hated killing. He hated himself when he was forced to take another life. But he did what had to be done in order to survive. If it meant someone else's life rather than his, especially if that life was evil or was trying to do him harm, then so be it. At this moment, he didn't think about his morals or about his pride. He needed to strike back, to preserve himself, and to protect his loved one.

He couldn't remember pulling the trigger. All he knew was that he was standing over the body of Haynes, which was riddled with bullet holes. The gun was on the floor, smoke drifting up from the barrel.

He had no time for remorse. He needed to move fast. To finish what had been started.

18

Sitting upon his mount, Petrie watched as the other horses ran into the distance. He had no more use for them. Haynes was as good as dead. The gunshots confirmed his intuition.

He waited a good distance from the building. Knowing Morgan, he would try to kill him. He was too far away for Morgan to aim accurately in his condition. In a while, he could go in and gather the body. It might take the rest of the night and into the morning, but time would win out.

19

Morgan peered out at Petrie through a crack in a wall. He was feeling very weak now. There was no way to get to him without Petrie seeing him. The only way would be to draw Petrie back to the building, but that would be impossible.

Thinking was cloudy. He forced the thoughts to fight their way through the murk in his mind.

He couldn't let it end this way!

20

The sun was going down. It was a long ride back home, but Petrie was confident he could find his way back. When he returned, he would reclaim Caroline with no resistance.

Some movement beyond a window caught his eye.

"Ya know," he yelled to the building. "I think I've changed my mind! I'm gonna go ahead and leave. There's no sense waiting around for you to die. That'll happen if I'm here or not. You're not going anywhere."

A figure was at the door. It hobbled out.

Petrie scratched his head, grimacing. What was that lunatic doing now? He cocked his gun, just to be sure.

"I want to talk to you," Morgan's weak voice drifted to him. "Don't let it end this way."

"You're not in much position to do anything about it."

"I'm dying. At least give me the dignity to die like a man."

"No." Petrie aimed the gun.

Morgan fell.

Petrie lowered the gun. He assumed this was a trick, but

was curious to see what Morgan had up his sleeve. He rounded his horse close to Morgan, revolver ready to shoot at any sign of movement.

Morgan was motionless. His eyes stared up at the sky, locked in a frozen gaze. One hand was buried underneath him and the other clutched the board that he had used as a crutch.

Petrie couldn't tell if he was breathing or not. If this was a trick, it was a poor one. He decided to leave. Let him lay out here for the buzzards to eat.

Just as he pulled back on the reins, a gunshot rang out, aimed elsewhere. Morgan was still motionless. Instead, the bullet blazed across the sand, away from him, erupting a line of cloud like a demonic mole.

Petrie was confused, thinking it was a misfire, when his horse reared up, throwing him roughly to the hard-packed dirt.

The horse bolted.

Petrie pulled himself up.

Morgan rose.

Petrie reached for his gun, now lying on the ground where it fell.

Morgan swung his crutch upward. His face was contorted in tortuous pain. He flung himself forward.

The pointed, ragged end of the crutch found its mark.

Morgan collapsed over the fallen body of Petrie, weeping.

It was over.

21

The horse did not run far after being spooked. It was a good mount. It stayed near its master. When it returned, Morgan was waiting for it.

Morgan could barely hold on when he pulled himself onto the horse's back. He sprawled over the saddle, breathing harshly. He prodded the horse with his good foot, prompting it to trot away from the mission.

He didn't know if the horse would find its way back home. He didn't know if he'd live if it did.

But it was over.

KNEE-DEEP

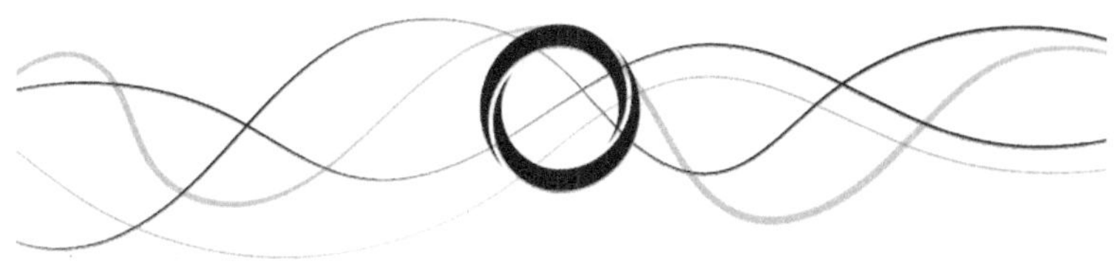

Dirt was everywhere. Under my fingernails. In my eyes. Between my teeth. A layer of soil lacquered my tongue, making even the air that passed through my mouth taste like a potted plant.

As slow realization overcame me, I noticed my repetitive actions. My sore arms thrust the shovel into the hard ground, scooped out a heaping helping, and tossed the payload onto a hefty pile next to the hole in which I stood. How did it get that large? I had only a ghost memory of digging, but did not understand why I was doing this. I only knew that I *had* to do it—the compulsion overrode logic.

Weariness latched onto my pitiful body. I collapsed into a sitting position on the edge of the hole. It was roughly circular, about five feet in diameter. The depth was a couple of feet. I tried to discern its purpose. If it was a grave, it would have been rectangular. Was I searching for buried treasure?

Still, musty air sat on my shoulders like a dead weight. I wiped sweat from my filthy brow that was caused by exertion despite the cool temperature. Breathing was labored, my lungs protesting their own workout.

I looked around at my surrounding, or at least as much as I could in the darkness. Vague walls stood just beyond my vision, but if I squinted, I could barely make out a faint solidity of what I thought was concrete. A black void hovered above me that was surely a ceiling, but its building material was beyond me. I determined I was in some sort of root cellar. I definitely was not digging for potatoes.

Urgency propelled me to continue digging. Ignoring my screaming muscles, I removed more and more earth, adding to the pile, adding to the hole.

Fragments of terror shot through me—of what, I could not say. I just knew that it was of utmost importance that I find whatever was hidden below this stagnant crypt.

A memory of this place zapped my brain. It was a farm owned by my grandparents, purchased sometime in the '50s. We would take refuge in the root cellar if the weather threatened to drop tornadoes from the sky. My grandpa was one to be prepared for all conditions.

I had gotten a phone call. Yes, that prompted the excursion out here. It was a long drive, but one that would save my life. Who was the call from?

Some people would think that I had little to live for. I was divorced and had no children—the doctors could never find a reason for our lack of procreation, but my ex blamed me as she did with pretty much everything. My lack of education and go-nowhere job kept me with little money. I had a couple of drinking buddies, but none who I would consider close friends. All-in-all, my entire existence was completely forgettable.

But it was mine, and I didn't want to give it up without a fight.

I retract my earlier statement. I had one close friend—or used to, anyway. He was my best friend in high school, but he joined the Army after graduating and we went separate ways. Rich tried to convince me to enlist, but I just couldn't see myself as a soldier. He made a career of it and ended up as a high-level functionary at the Pentagon. I received Christmas and birthday cards from him every year, and every so often we'd talk on the phone and catch up. His stories were ultimately more exciting than mine—at least the ones he could talk about—but he always pretended to be interested in the mundane facts about my life.

A splinter from the wooden shovel handle speared into my hand, sliding under several layers of skin. I sucked on the wound, tasting the bitter grime that coated my hand. I couldn't let something this minor stop my endeavor.

I always wondered how many people would show up at my funeral if I died today. My ex might arrive in a party dress. A couple of guys from work might drop in for a few minutes to pay their respects. My sister in Tulsa might begrudgingly work it into her busy schedule. The few cousins I have would most likely send flowers if they acknowledged the occasion at all.

Would I go to any of their funerals? Probably. It was something to do. Though I won't have to worry about that now.

The phone conversation came back to me. It was Rich, sounding unlike himself. His voice was hitching, as if he was crying. "I just needed to tell someone," he explained. "I couldn't live with myself if I didn't." He laughed ironically.

"What is it?" Fear gripped my chest, but it was nothing like what I would soon experience—fear that would temporarily blank my memory.

"The missiles are flying. They'll be hitting their targets within the hour."

"How could this happen? I thought the threat of nuclear war was behind us."

He had no answer to that. All he could say was, "You were a good friend. I thought I owed it to you to tell you before it's too late."

Then I remembered the old farm. I raced out here in a panic, and in my frenzy instinct took over. I suppose it's an ancient survival mechanism lying dormant in human DNA.

The tip of the shovel clanged against metal. I doubled my effort to clear the dirt, exposing a hatch. We all thought my grandfather's bomb shelter was quaint, though he treated it with deathly seriousness. Eventually, the entry was buried and forgotten.

Almost.

I yanked on the lever. It moved a bit, but being long-unused kept it frozen. I knew I was running out of time, so I worked at it until it finally slid aside. The heavy lid creaked open.

That is when I heard it—a distant whistle, like an incoming mortar as depicted in old war movies, or maybe a jet engine whirring up to speed.

I dropped into the gaping maw and pulled the hatch closed behind me.

The explosion was nothing like what I expected. Even

buried in the ground, the concussion shook the shelter like a hound dog with a rabbit. I fell unconscious, and when I regained my senses, my ears were muffled to even the sound of my own voice. There was absolutely no light, so I was totally blind. I felt around and found bare shelves.

What kind of world I would find when I emerged from my sanctuary? I could not even comprehend. How much longer would I last? How would I survive? Would I find anyone else alive?

All I knew was now life meant something, and I wasn't about to throw it away.

THE MUSICIAN

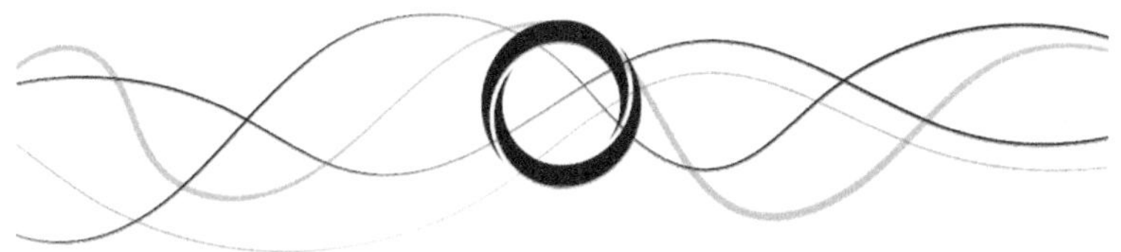

Every day, Kyle passed by the old mill that sat at the top of the rocky waterfall, which formed the head of the Linden River. Every day, he heard sweet music drift through the leaves of the surrounding trees and would pause for a moment on his way home from school to listen. The ethereal melody lingered in the air just long enough for him to savor its flavor before fading into wisps of wind chimes and birdsong.

No one ever heard the music except for Kyle. He learned a long time ago not to mention it to anyone or he would invite ridicule from his peers. After first hearing the beautiful song, he brought two of his school friends to the mill to listen. He heard it for a moment, but his friends did not. They made fun of him, accused him of imagining things. That did not sit well with him and two bloody noses resulted. Unfortunately, one belonged to him.

He also mentioned it to his parents one day, several

weeks after first hearing the music. He had wondered if he indeed was hearing things. His father brushed it off as childhood imaginings while his mother told him not to be playing around that old mill. He even brought his little brother out there once, but again Kyle was the only one to hear the tune that seemed to play at the edge of his audible range. His brother thought he was a little odd, but that was nothing new.

Kyle had first heard the enchanting music early in the spring. It was now fall, nearing winter, and all the leaves had changed to their respective oranges and reds and yellows. The wind blew chilly, the sun only heating the air during the mid-day when there were no clouds in the sky. Snow would be falling soon, then another year would pass. This saddened Kyle, for he wanted time to stand still and every moment to stretch out for eternity. To his dismay, he found time slipping by, events gradually becoming lost in the frail memory of bygone days.

He stood leaning against an old railing, looking at the old mill with fondness. The music faded, just as it always did, but still he remained, losing himself in that wonderful place that his mind liked to take him, searching out the possibilities that existed inside his mind yet seemed so real in his heart.

The mill had been standing for an eternity, had been around since the first settlers of the town called this stretch of land home. It was one of two buildings which still stood from that era. The other was the corner building on Main Street and Grand Avenue, which was remodeled ten years ago and now held a real estate agency and a video rental store. The old mill had gone out of commission ages ago, and no one had much interest in either preserving it or tearing it down. So now it stood, decrepit and wasted, but somehow magical and special. It was as if it belonged in that condition, iconic to the town.

Kyle turned to go, hands shoved down deep in his jacket pockets, head dropping as he stared at his feet. Something caught his ear and he stopped to listen. Sure enough, he heard it. The melody had returned.

He rushed back to his spot by the fence, his personal place to listen to the music. The music always came to him just once in each day. This was the first time it had come to him a second time.

Closing his eyes, he concentrated on the beauty that melted into his ears. This was indeed something special, although he didn't know why it was singing out to him a second time today.

The song was barely audible over the wind, which was picking up intensity, rustling noisily through the colored leaves about him. But it was there. Oh yes, it was there.

He wondered, not for the first time, what evoked the melodies. He knew there were several instruments and he could count at least three at any single time, though he had discovered at least a dozen distinct sounds during his time as its sole audience. None of the instruments were recognizable to him, but many were very familiar. Some were like wood-winds, while others were definitely strings. A couple of brass instruments piped in often and at least one chime turned up now and again.

It wasn't always the same song which he heard, but the melodies were always very similar. Just as the instruments varied, so did the music itself, with different tempos and different arrangements. Some days it was light and playful, while other days it was dramatic and powerful. But it was always beautiful.

This time, this special encore performance, the music was sorrowful. It sang of hurt and loss within its woeful chords. Kyle's heart felt ready to break. It was as if the entire world was crying out in emotional pain, and it pulled him into its suffering. He wanted the sorrow to end, but he didn't want to turn away from the music. It was his gift, and no matter how tragic or painful, he would not turn away from it. He would accept it, embrace it. Without an audience, the music was wasted.

Realizing his eyes had been closed for some time, Kyle opened them and looked upon the old mill as he had done in the many months since the music first appeared. Only this time, the mill seemed different. He couldn't say exactly how. It was still falling apart from disuse, set back in the overgrown vegetation near the water spilling over the rocks from the moldy mill pond. But something was different about it, like a different light was shining on it.

The music still played, but it changed subtly. It was still very sad, but not as desperate, and seemed to compel him. It wanted him; it wanted him to join the creator of the music.

A warm chill ran throughout his body, and suddenly he felt tiny. It was time. The music wanted him. It was as if he had walked through a door to find a vast landscape spread out at his feet. He was a tiny part of the universe, and now was his time to stand before its majesty.

He felt the urge to turn and run, but he knew he could never do that. The music was his, and likewise, he belonged to the music. The past three seasons were just a preparation for this moment. It wanted him, and he was giving himself to it.

Kyle stepped forward, through the brittle, dry weeds which populated the mill's lawn. Harsh, purple flowers bent on their stiff stalks as his sneakers cautiously stepped forward. In all the time he stopped here, not once did he actually approach the mill. The thought occurred to him once or twice, but he didn't feel it was right. Before, it was okay to look at the old mill from the roadside but not to get any closer. Now, he was expected to enter it.

He felt lightheaded; the world swaying gently before his eyes. The atmosphere about him was golden and misty, reminding him of those sappy long-distance telephone commercials. He drew a deep breath, and felt cool, clean air rush into his lungs, filling his veins with immaculate oxygen.

The boards under his feet squeaked loudly as he stepped onto the porch. He knew no one would hear and took no mind.

Kyle inspected the wood which remained of the building. It was not only old, but ancient, timeless. The mill was not a mere hundred years old, not even two hundred. It was eternal. It had rested on this land since the soil it sat upon first came into being. And before that, it still existed, somewhere, in some other form.

A thrill of anticipation shuddered his young body as he pushed open the door. It barely turned on its rusted hinge, grinding the oxidized metal into a fine powder which floated into the air in a red cloud.

He couldn't keep his foot from quaking as he placed it inside the doorway. His breath came in shallow sputters. He sucked on his lips. One foot was in, so now he just had to pull in the rest of him. He just had to—

He was in.

Amazement washed over Kyle. He was standing inside the mill. He recognized the structure and the architecture. But it was not the mill. In fact, Kyle wondered if he was still in the same world. He felt as if he wore kaleidoscopes over his eyes. He was sure the universe had tilted, so that reality skewed into a distortion of sanity.

The sensation was overwhelming and he swooned. Luckily, he steadied himself with a nearby wooden beam that wasn't quite wood.

Kyle squeezed his eyes shut, thinking that in his excitement, too much blood had rushed to his head, causing temporary delirium. Taking a deep breath, he re-opened his eyes.

The world had steadied itself, but it was still altered into that non-reality. This time, however, it did not bother him. As he became used to the strangeness of it all, he saw the wonder of this alternative universe. He couldn't help but walk around, taking in every detail. The thrill and excitement filled him with fresh energy and he quickened his pace, trying to learn everything he could about this fantastic place.

He had almost forgotten the reason he was here when a voice spoke to him.

"Hello there, young man. Finding my home interesting?"

Kyle froze where he stood. Guilt overtook him as he thought he had trespassed into someone's private property. He shook that thought out of his head quickly. He knew better. Perhaps it was a vagabond taking shelter in the old mill. Except this wasn't the old mill, not really.

"Don't worry. You're in no harm," the voice said again. It was a kindly voice, one that Kyle could trust.

A man stepped out of a deep shadow. He was perhaps as tall as Kyle himself, with a sturdy and stout frame that carried no excess weight. He was bald on top, his pate wreathed with long, flowing jet black hair which merged with his equally long beard. This combination made his head look bell-shaped. He wore a wide grin, which split the beard pleasantly. His eyes danced on sparks of light.

"Your name, I believe, is Kyle," the funny small man said grandly. His voice was not deep, but it had resonance and lilted melodically.

"Yes," Kyle said, clearing his throat, which suddenly became clogged. "How'd you know?"

"I should know the name of my friend who visits me every day."

"What else do you know about me?"

"Not much. You mean personal stuff like what your favorite food is and what your family does on weekend outings and things like that? I really don't need to know all that. But I know what is important."

"What's important?" This man intrigued Kyle, and the boy actually felt very comfortable in his company.

"Well...that you hear the music. That's important."

"What's so important about it?"

"The music is very special, and only a few people may hear it. You are one of the lucky few."

"So other people can hear it!" That answered one of his questions.

"Yes, but most prefer not to hear it."

"Why?"

"I can't answer that. They have their own reasons, I suppose. It takes more than the ability, it takes the desire. Unfortunately, desire is not something that is as easily accessible."

"Oh." Kyle didn't quite understand what the man was talking about, but he would go along with him. "What's your name?"

"Guildermile."

"That's a strange name."

"No stranger than Kyle," Guildermile said with a corner of his mouth crooked upwardly.

"I guess not," Kyle shrugged. "Who are you?"

"Don't you know?"

"You're the musician!"

"Quite right."

"But why do you make that music all the time?"

"Why not?"

That seemed an obvious, though unsatisfying, answer.

"This is all so strange," said Kyle. He sat down on the wooden beam and gazed around the majestic room once again. He was warming up to this place, although he was more confused than before.

"You are just unfamiliar with this part of the world."

"So this is still on Earth?"

Guildermile let out a cheerful, heartfelt laugh. "Oh yes, we're still on Earth. We're in the old mill, silly!"

"I don't understand. It's so different."

"Yes, it is different. Only because you're reaching a new level of understanding. Soon it will be quite different again."

"Why?"

"Why why why? I'd forgotten how the youth is filled with questions. But all the better. The moment you stop asking questions is the time you die."

"My mom gets mad when I ask so many questions. My dad just ignores me."

"That's because they no longer see the world through young eyes. But they have questions of their own they pose. Questions that nobody but they can answer."

"You don't make much sense."

Again, Guildermile laughed. His laughter was addictive, and Kyle giggled alongside his companion.

"The music!" Kyle exclaimed after regaining control of himself. He realized with a start that the music was no longer playing.

"Don't worry. It is still playing, but right now...for someone else."

"You mean it moves around to different people?"

"I told you only a few hear the music. They don't all hear the same song. Each song is designed especially for a particular person. You only hear your song, and no one else hears it."

"Neat."

"The music is very frail, and overexposure must be avoided. Even I don't hear my song all the time."

"You have your own song, too?"

"Naturally! What's a musician without a song?"

"I thought you made the music."

"Oh no. It's not in my power to create it. I'm only a tool to send the music out into the world. I craft it, mold it into something that people can understand and enjoy. I am but a humble servant."

"Who do you serve?"

"I don't think I have to answer that question."

"Why do you—"

"I am very sorry, but I'm afraid I must attend to my work," Guildermile said with a compassionate smile. "I can't get behind or I'll never get caught up. One must stay on tempo, you know."

"But what about me?"

"Go on home. I'll be here tomorrow. When you hear the music, come in."

Guildermile winked, then Kyle felt dizziness grab hold of him. He steadied himself, then found himself back at the fence. His world had returned to him, and it was a disappointment.

KYLE WAS DISTRACTED AT DINNER THAT NIGHT. HIS MOTHER inquired about his health and he said he felt fine. Later, he had a hard time falling asleep. His mind kept returning him to the old mill, that alternate old mill, and he wondered if he hadn't imagined the whole thing.

School the next day was difficult. Concentrating on the teachers' lectures was difficult, and he felt nervous and antsy all day.

Once last bell of the afternoon rang, Kyle wasted no time returning to the mill. It was a cloudy, drizzly day.

A sullenness draped over him. He didn't meet anyone in

there yesterday—it had been a dream or a hallucination, and the music never existed. He was losing his mind.

He half-convinced himself of this and considered leaving when the music arrived. It was a slow but cheerful variation of the tune, in sharp contrast with the mood of the afternoon sky. It made him feel happy, wanted, and he knew it was real, that Guildermile was real and waited for him just inside the building.

Kyle wasn't nervous this time. He was eager to see the funny little man again. He hurried across the overgrown yard and through the front door. That unsettling sensation returned, but he wasn't frightened of it this time. He actually found it rather fun.

Opening his eyes, he saw the room was empty. His music was still playing. He walked about, looking for Guildermile. The shadowy areas were quite larger than first impressions appeared. Shadows led to what looked like entirely new rooms. The mill was like a funhouse, never knowing where the next doorway would lead. Kyle guessed that with every turn, wonderful surprises awaited an adventurous youth such as himself.

The music slowly faded out. It never finished with a definite conclusion. It always just disappeared. Kyle supposed if it ever concluded, it would never play for him again.

"Hello, my young friend!" Guildermile's voice called out from apparently nowhere.

"Hi," Kyle replied. "Where are you?"

"Over here." Kyle knew exactly where the voice was coming from. He walked across the room and through an archway of fallen lumber. The shadow engulfed him for a moment.

Kyle stood in a wondrous, brightly colored studio filled with gadgets that he could only guess at their purpose. Guildermile was hunched over an oddity and looked up when Kyle entered.

"And how are you today?" The musician bobbed his head.

"Okay."

"One must never be just 'okay.' To be 'okay' designates the absence of emotions. Without emotions, one is no longer human."

Kyle frowned, not knowing how to respond.

"How do you like my workshop?" Guildermile asked, hopping upon a table.

"What are all these things?" Kyle asked.

"Just some contraptions to help me in my work. They really are quite handy sometimes, but they're very temperamental. I'm always tweaking them here and there, adjusting this, revising that. But it keeps me busy."

"Are you all alone?"

"The entire world keeps me company."

"I mean, doesn't anyone live with you?"

"No, I live here by myself."

"Don't you get lonely?"

Guildermile took a deep breath and let it out, smiling. "When you have important work to do, sometimes you are too busy to worry about such things. But other times, when you do something exciting and exhilarating, you want to rush to a loved one to share your new discovery. When there's no one there to share it with, then yes, it is lonely."

"I'm glad I could come and visit," Kyle said. The thought of being here all alone, even if it was such a wonderful place, saddened him. It occurred to him that his life wasn't much different from Guildermile's. He had no close friends, and just a few kids at school hung around him when it suited them. His parents often treated him like he was an intrusion and a bother. He knew they loved him, but either they were indifferent to him or they scolded him. Nothing he ever did seemed important to them. None of his problems or ideas were real to them. He knew about loneliness. His bedroom often was more isolated from humanity than this old mill.

The musician smiled. "I, too, am glad you are here. However, this is no visit."

"What do you mean?" Kyle didn't like the sound of that.

"I mean, you are not here for pleasure. Much work is to be done, and you must begin your training now."

"My training? What are you talking about?"

"Do you think I am going to hold this position forever?"

"Sending out the music to the world?"

"Precisely."

"I don't know. I didn't think about it. I didn't know this was just a job."

"Oh, it's not just a job, not as you conceive it. I wasn't the first to hold this duty, and I most certainly won't be the last. I must train an apprentice to take over when my time is finished."

"You want me as your apprentice?" Kyle was flabbergasted.

"It is not a question of my wants," Guildermile replied. "You were chosen."

"By who? I don't understand this!"

"Many things exist in this universe that I don't understand. And yet I follow the rules just the same."

"This is really confusing. I think I'd better go home—" Kyle stepped backward and stumbled over a strange object that lit up with a multitude of colors when it hit the ground.

Guildermile sighed and picked up the object and brushed it off.

"Sorry," Kyle replied, embarrassed.

"You do not have to do anything you don't wish to do. You can't be forced into this. It must be of your own choosing. If you decide against the apprenticeship, another will accept it. But you heard the music, and you responded. The position is yours for the taking."

KYLE ATE NOTHING THAT NIGHT. HIS MOTHER WAS CERTAIN HE WAS sick. He looked very flushed and his temperature was a little high. She kept him home from school the next morning and he stayed in his room all day.

He had a lot to think about—the decision was overwhelming. It wasn't fair, choosing him like this with no warning. What did he know about music? He didn't even play an instrument. His parents thought the school band was a waste of time and money. How was he expected to drop everything and move away from home to live in that mill forever?

And yet...the offer was tempting. Being in the mill made him feel like he was floating in the clouds. It was a wonderful place, one he wouldn't mind living his whole life in. And there were enough surprises in it to last a lifetime. It was a secret doorway that only he knew...a doorway to another world, or at least a part of this one that no one ever saw. Except him.

Kyle often wondered what it would be like to run away from home and live on his own, to head into the wilderness and live off the land with nothing to worry about except what directly affected him. No parental authority to deal with, no school to worry about. He would be alone.

The idea was romantic, but he knew it was unrealistic. He could no more live off the land than he could fly. He wouldn't have TV, or his mother's cooking, or his bed. Life would be difficult.

But now he had another choice.

"Why did you choose to be a musician?"

"I didn't choose. It was chosen of me."

"You know what I mean," Kyle said, slightly annoyed at Guildermile's avoiding his questions.

"I gave up a family, you know," the little man said, his tone turning serious. "Had a wife and two daughters. They haven't seen me since I took the position."

Kyle was aghast. He could understand escaping the authority of parents, but to abandon a family?

"You just left?" Kyle asked. "Did you even say goodbye?"

"In a manner of speaking." Guildermile seemed far off, distant. "They sensed something was wrong, but I assured them that everything was okay."

"Okay! How could everything be okay? Two little girls! Their father was deserting them!"

"No, not deserting them! I have been with them every day of their lives. I have watched them grow, get married, have children of their own...and grow old and die."

"I...I don't understand." Guildermile couldn't be that old. He couldn't have been much older than Kyle's own father.

"Come here." Guildermile led Kyle through a previously unnoticed doorway and took him down a long hallway, which opened into a dimly lit room. A roundish object filled with smoky lights sat in the center of the room that reminded Kyle of the witch's crystal ball in The Wizard of Oz, except this one appeared to be electronic.

As they approached, an image appeared through the cloudy glass. A man, a woman, and two little girls appeared in the magical television. Kyle didn't recognize any of them.

"I could watch over them at all times," Guildermile said quietly. "I could never directly affect their lives, but I could influence them with the music. I gave them inspiration and hope, and helped them through their troubled times and remained helpless when they made mistakes."

"Who's the guy?"

"It would be unfair to leave them without a father. He became their father in my absence. My little girls...their memory of me was erased." He paused, as if on the verge of an emotional outburst, but quickly regained control of himself. "He has been a good father."

Kyle didn't know what to say. He looked upon Guildermile with new respect and curiosity. What would make someone leave his wife and children and let them forget he ever existed? Was the music that important to him? Was it that important to the world?

His thought turned inward, and he wondered about himself. He was now faced with making a similar decision. What was he to do?

Guildermile placed a hand on the boy's shoulder and smiled warmly. "I wouldn't want it any other way. Through me, millions of people are filled with emotion, inspired to do great things, and moved in ways I can't comprehend. I was the instrument for many wonderful things. My family didn't suffer. Yes, I have been lonely many times. Yet, the entire world is at my hands. I am proud of my job, but it is nearing an end. If I do not have a replacement, it would be tragic."

"I don't know anything about what you do. You can't expect me to take over just like that."

"No, I can't. You shall be my apprentice until you are ready. Then I will pass the instruments over to you. That is how it happened with me, how it has always happened. You have nothing to fear."

As Kyle walked home, the music followed him. This was the first time it played beyond the reach of the mill. He wondered if it was trying to influence him, or if this was a natural progression of the music.

After a while, it faded away, but he knew it would return.

He contemplated the possibility of hearing it all the

time, controlling it, giving it to others to hear. What a gift to share!

That night, he watched his mother and father as they went about their routine. He wondered if they would miss him.

How could they miss him, he scolded himself, if they didn't even remember that he existed?

Kyle pictured life in this house without him, with another boy, another son, in his place. What would his alternate look like? Would his name be Kyle, or would he be a totally different person? Would his parents be happier with his replacement?

And what of his own life? Would he continue to age normally? Would he grow up or forever stay a child? Guildermile spoke as if he was hundreds of years old, though he didn't look it.

How long would Guildermile's tutoring last? Would it go by quickly or would it seem like forever? What would life be like after Guildermile left?

Most importantly, did Kyle want the job?

He lay awake all night pondering these questions and dreaming up new ones. It was scary.

How could he say yes?

How could he say no?

THE NEXT MORNING, HIS MOTHER ASKED HIM IF HE WAS FEELING sick. He didn't look well. His father even noticed that there was something troubling him.

Kyle's response was, "Nothing is the matter. I love you."

As he walked out the front door, he glanced back over his shoulder for one last look at his parents, and for the first time, he realized they were truly wonderful people. He knew they would continue their lives without interruption.

Kyle was embarking on a voyage that would transport him to faraway lands and introduce him to a variety of people, and he would learn things far beyond his imagination. He could touch the hearts and souls of people everywhere.

He would be a musician.

AFTERWORD

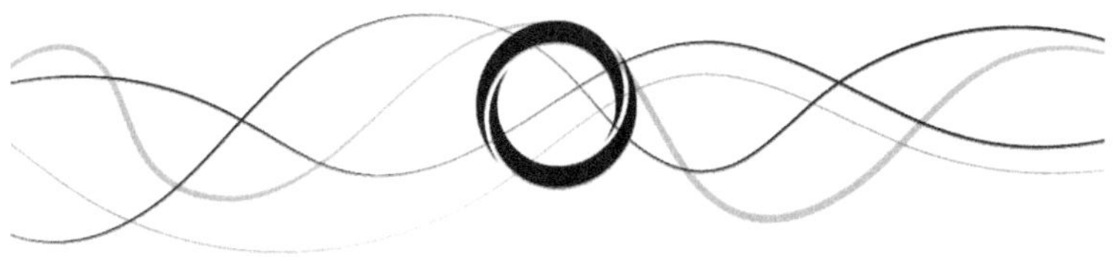

Many thanks go to the Panhandle Writers Group in Milton, Florida. My participation in it is the reason that many of the stories featured in this volume exist and why I felt compelled to put them together in an anthology.

I naturally also need to thank my parents for their constant, unwavering support and my friends and family for their encouragement and positive words, even when they're often bombarded by an endless stream of story ideas.

This book is dedicated to the late Bruce White, Sr. He was married to my mom's sister, and I spent a good deal of my childhood in his presence. Many of my summers were spent with my aunt and uncle, a time I cherish. He was full of a lot of wild ideas that sparked my imagination. I can vividly remember having long, in-depth conversations with him on topics both serious and fantastical. Obviously, the opening story, "The Portals," was inspired by my relationship with him, though of course highly fictionalized. He's been gone a good decade and a half now, but I still miss him.

I'm not going to explain where I got the ideas for all the stories in this book—to some degree, revealing the *why* behind it ruins the story. Many people expect a certain type of story from me because of my attraction to science fiction and horror; in fact, more than a few people advised me to compile stories only of a certain genre. But doesn't that detract from the wonderment of the surprise? There's a certain joy in not knowing what to expect from moment to moment. After all, who would expect a western in this anthology after reading what preceded it?

That said, I will address one entry—the poem, "Never Forget." Poetry is an art form that I respect, but am rarely moved to write. In this instance, it was the only way to express what I was feeling.

Like much of our country, and probably the world, I watched the events of September 11, 2001 unfold on live television. No fiction can come close to the horror that we shared. I can only imagine what it was like to have actually been in New York on that day. Regardless, that senseless tragedy had such a powerful impact on me, I honestly don't know if I will ever completely exorcise it from my soul. In the years after, with two middle-eastern wars, the Patriot Act, natural disasters, seemingly unending examples of racism and other forms of bigotry, political hatred, economic upheaval, and insanity in the media, it makes me wonder if our society will ever improve. Yet, somehow, I still have hope. Call me the eternal optimist.

Perhaps I should mention that one of these stories is not entirely fictional and is based on an actual experience. I won't say which one, but it's not too hard to figure out (hint: it's not the zombie story).

One last note—sharp readers may have realized that both the opening and closing stories feature a young man who faces a choice whether to leave his family for grander adventures. In the former, the protagonist chooses to stay and continue to live his normal life; in the latter, our hero decides to give up everything he knows in order to move on to a larger purpose and face mysteries yet undiscovered. I rather like the idea of leaving you, the reader, facing the unknown.

Sometimes, there's no place like home—but where would we be if we never journeyed over the rainbow?

ABOUT THE AUTHOR

Stephen Wise is a multiple award-winning screenwriter and filmmaker with a Bachelor's degree in film production from the University of Central Florida. His films have been screened in over a dozen countries. He is the co-writer of *Batman: DarKnight*, which IFC hailed as one of the seven best unproduced Batman screenplays. He is a Michigan native and currently resides in Northwest Florida.

To find out more about Stephen Wise and his work, visit StephenJWise.com

amazon.com/stores/Stephen-Wise/author/B00R25T4YY

facebook.com/stephenwisefilmmaker

threads.net/@stephenjwise

linkedin.com/in/stephenjwise

bsky.app/profile/stephenjwise.bsky.social

instagram.com/stephenwiseauthor

goodreads.com/stephenwise

ARROWHEAD PUBLICATIONS

If you enjoyed this book, be sure to write a review of it on your favorite platform to help other people discover it.

To learn more about Arrowhead Publications and its books, visit arrowheadpublications.com or scan the QR code to go to the website.

Follow us on social media.

facebook.com/arrowheadpublications

instagram.com/arrowheadpublications

threads.net/@arrowheadpublications

bsky.app/profile/arrowheadpubs.bsky.social

www.ingramcontent.com/pod-product-compliance
Lightning Source LLC
Chambersburg PA
CBHW020805310726

48969CB00002B/714